RUNNER

HARRY JEROME, WORLD'S FASTEST MAN

Red Deer Press

NORMA CHARLES

Red Deer Press, 195 Allstate Parkway, Markham, ON L3R 4T8
Published in Canada by Red Deer Press

Published in the United States by Red Deer Press
311 Washington Street, Brighton, MA 02135

10 9 8 7 6 5 4 3 2 1

Red Deer Press acknowledges with thanks the Canada Council for the Arts and the Ontario Arts Council for their support of our publishing program. We acknowledge the financial support of the Government of Canada through the Canada Book Fund (CBF) for our publishing activities.

ONTARIO ARTS COUNCIL
CONSEIL DES ARTS DE L'ONTARIO
an Ontario government agency
un organisme du gouvernement de l'Ontario

Canada Council   Conseil des arts
for the Arts   du Canada

Library and Archives Canada Cataloguing in Publication

Charles, Norma M., author
Runner : Harry Jerome, world's fastest
man / Norma Charles.
ISBN 978-0-88995-553-0 (softcover)
1. Jerome, Harry, 1940-1982--Juvenile fiction.
I. Title.
Publisher Cataloging-in-Publication Data (U.S.)

Names: Charles, Norma M., author.
Title: Runner : Harry Jerome, World's Fastest Man / Norma Charles.
Description: Markham, Ontario : Red Deer Press, 2017. | Summary: "Based on the real life, true story of Harry Jerome, 'fastest man on earth', African-American, forgotten Canadian icon, athletic hero and role model, this inspirational novel of hope and diversity details his rise to running glory against all odds, including challenges of racism and prejudice in the 1950s and 1960s" – Provided by publisher.

Identifiers: ISBN 978-0-88995-553-0 (paperback)
Subjects: LCSH: Jerome, Harry. | African American athletes – Biography -- Juvenile fiction. | Racism – Juvenile fiction. | Runners (Sports) – Juvenile fiction. | BISAC: YOUNG ADULT FICTION / Historical / Canada.
Classification: LCCPZ7.C437Ru | DDC [F] – dc23

Edited for the Press by Peter Carver
Interior and cover design by Tanya Montini

Cover image of Harry Jerome statue, Vancouver, courtesy of Nick Kenrick Photography, Victoria, Canada. Nick's work can be found at www.redbubble and on flickr.com

Printed in Canada

For my grandsons, Elijah and Kai,
two brilliant runners

PREFACE

This is a story I've wanted to write for over fifty years, ever since the early 1960s when I first saw Harry Jerome run. At the time I was engaged to Trinidadian Carlos Charles who was a sprinter at UBC so, of course, I went to all the track meets. And that's where I met Harry. At that first track meet, although my memory may be faulty, I remember Carlos beating Harry in the 100 yards and the 200.

But it soon became clear that this "kid" from North Van was no ordinary runner. Harry was a *serious* runner. He was in it to *win*. And soon, win he did, race after race. Not only was he winning, but he did it with what seemed to be a completely effortless stride. We were amazed that he wasn't even winded at the end of his races. That young fellow had determination. He had drive. Sometimes, he struck us as being quiet, shy, reserved. Not "one of the guys" like his good friend, Paul Winn, who was also part of the track community. Paul always had a joke to tell and a big hearty laugh.

At the time, I wondered about Harry. He hadn't come from the West Indies as had many young people in track. Where was he from? What was his background? Where did he get that drive, that determination? What had brought him to the point of becoming one of the fastest runners in Canada? In the world?

I met his sister, Valerie, around that time. She was a young teen also enthusiastic about track. Both she and Harry were with the Vancouver Striders track team coached by John Minichiello.

Carlos and I were married in 1961 and he left the track scene behind. But we both continued to follow Harry's story with great interest as he went from triumph to defeat, then back to triumph again. Carlos and I raised four children, all of whom were keen about track and field and joined the local track club, the Jericho Jaguars. I have always felt that their devotion to track helped pull them through the teenage years. During those years at track events, we occasionally bumped into both Harry and Valerie, and of course, John Minichiello.

A couple of years ago, it hit me that although there was a magnificent bronze statue of Harry in Stanley Park to commemorate his achievements, as well as a large Harry Jerome

Sports Complex in North Vancouver, some people, especially young people, didn't even know who Harry Jerome was. There were no books for children about this great Canadian hero. None. In fact, there are very few books for children about *any* Afro-Canadians.

My children, my grandchildren, needed a book about this Canadian hero.

I met with Valerie who generously shared with me stories about their childhood. I also met with Paul Winn who said that he still misses Harry every day, even though it's been thirty-five years since Harry died. John Minichiello gave me a detailed account of coaching this gifted athlete.

I'm interested in the connection between what people go through as children and who they become as adults. I thought about the sheer persistence it took Harry, so terribly injured, and then maligned as a runner by the press, and still having the strength to train so hard that he won a gold medal in the British Empire Games in Jamaica. That achievement would never have been possible if he hadn't already conquered huge obstacles and setbacks in childhood. Most people would have simply given up. But not our Harry. He was drawing upon a reservoir of enormous inner strength and fortitude many of us could never imagine.

I believe passionately that all children need to see role models in their lives so they can picture themselves as successful adults someday in whatever way of life they choose. I've written this book especially for my own children and grandchildren so they can catch a glimpse of themselves as Canadians in the history of this multicultural country.

CHAPTER 1

The night of May 5, 1950, would be burnt into Harry Jerome's memory forever. It was probably his very first race. It happened when he was just nine years old.

That race was against the raging Red River near his home in St. Boniface, Manitoba, known as Winnipeg's French district. Harry was among many who tried to stop the river from overflowing its banks and flooding the city.

The evening started in the most ordinary way. Harry was sitting at the kitchen table after supper, reading his new Superman comic, when his mother called from her bedroom. "I'm getting up now and those dishes better be done." Her voice was scratchy, as if she were getting a cold.

The table was still cluttered with dirty dishes from their supper of wieners and beans. Harry sighed and wished he could have the exciting life of a superhero like Superman. He'd fly out there into the night and save mankind from destruction.

"It's your turn to wash, Carolyn," he told one of his sisters. Harry had two sisters, both younger than him. Carolyn was eight and Valerie six.

Carolyn was across the table from him, biting her lip as she concentrated on cutting out ladies from the thick Eaton's catalog with Mom's big kitchen scissors. Harry wondered how his sisters could play with boring cut-outs so much.

"No, it's not," Carolyn said. "I washed them last night. And you better get them done before Mom gets up. She'll be really mad when she sees this mess."

There was a loud knock at the back door. Harry could see through the window that it was his friend, Tommy, who lived down the street on Enfield Crescent.

"Hi, Tommy," he said, opening the door. "What's up?"

The cold wind blew in a wet draft of air.

Tommy LeBlanc's coat was wet and rain dripped from the brim of his cap. His round cheeks were red and he was breathing hard.

"Harry. You got to come. Right now. It's an emergency. Down at the river. All the cubs from our pack. Meeting there. To load sand into sandbags. For the dikes."

"All right! Tell Mom when she gets up," Harry called to his

sisters as he grabbed his coat and wooly hat off the hooks by the door and pulled on his rubber boots. "I have to go help the cub pack down at the river."

It was like his wish had come true. Maybe this was his chance to be a hero.

"But what about the dishes?" Carolyn called after him.

He didn't even answer. He pulled his coat closer against the wind. It had been raining like crazy all day. He followed Tommy, jogging down Enfield Crescent to Taché Avenue, which ran along the river bank. Harry squinted against the icy rain nipping his cheeks. Sure was a cold night. Like that rain wasn't just rain, but had icy needles mixed in. With the thick cloud cover, it was getting so dark he could barely see the river. But he sure could hear it. It was roaring past the riverbank like a freight train.

"Over here!" Mr. Comeau, his cub pack master waved. He was a friendly man with a bushy beard. They called him "Akela," the name given to adult leaders of a cub pack.

"Glad you could make it, fellows," he said.

Harry and Tommy joined a bunch of other nine- and ten-year-old cub scouts gathered around him.

"This is what we have to do," Akela said. "Here's a stack of gunnysacks. You guys fill them with sand from that pile over there as fast as you can. Then you carry the sacks across the road and hand them to one of the soldiers there who'll pile them up on the dike. Got it?"

The dike was a wall of sandbags the soldiers were constructing along the river's edge to try to stop the rising waters from overflowing the banks and flooding the city.

Tommy and Harry worked as a team. Tommy filled a sack with sand with a shovel while Harry held its gritty top open. Then Harry dragged the sack across the road as fast as he could to one of the soldiers. The soldier hoisted it up and piled it on top of the dike while Harry raced back to grab another sack. Other cubs were doing the same all along that section of the dike.

This was what a superhero would do. It was exciting and fun. A lot more fun than washing supper dishes, anyway. At least it was at first. But after a while, Harry got tired of hauling the bags across the road.

"Hey, kid," a tall soldier called out to him. "You sure that sack's not too heavy for you?"

"Nah," Harry said. "I can lift it." He tried to heave the sack up onto his shoulder to show how strong he was, even though he was on the small side for a nine-year-old. But his tired muscles protested and he stumbled.

"Okay. I got it." The soldier grinned at him and tossed the sack up onto the dike as if it was filled with fluffy feathers and not wet sand.

When Harry got back to the sand pile, he said, "Hey, Tommy. Want to switch jobs for a while?"

So Harry shoveled sand into the bags while Tommy tried to hurry across the road to the line of soldiers with them. He lasted only three runs.

"You got to do the running, Harry," he panted. "I can't keep up."

So they switched back. It was raining even harder now. And the rain was definitely mixed with snow. Harry wished he'd remembered his mitts. He pulled his coat sleeves over his throbbing fingers and grabbed another full bag of sand. He forced his tired muscles to drag it across the road, knowing Superman would think nothing of being a bit tired.

"Come on, fellows. The river's getting even higher," Akela yelled. "We need more bags. Hurry!"

The sound of the river roaring past the wall of sandbags grew louder. Harry pulled in a deep breath and raced across the street to drag another bag filled with sodden sand.

"Thanks, kid." The soldier grabbed the bag. He tossed it to the top of the dike and patted it into place. The dike was higher than Harry's shoulder now. In the dim light, he could see some river water was getting through, seeping through the lower layers of sandbags.

He ran back to fetch another bag. And another. And another. The boys and the soldiers, as well as fathers and mothers from the neighborhood, worked on relentlessly, far into the night. After a while, Harry felt like a machine. His hands, his arms, his whole body, were numb from cold and wet and exhaustion. But he just kept at his job: grab the filled sandbag, drag it across the road, heave it up to one of the soldiers, run back for the next bag. Cub scouts always did their best. That was their motto: "Do Your Best." They didn't quit, ever. And he was no quitter.

This had been a long hard winter on the prairies with more snow than usual. Then at the end of April, a sudden warm spell caused the ice on the river to break up. Meanwhile, all the winter's snow from the surrounding fields melted, and water streamed into the muddy Assiniboine and Red Rivers. As the water level rose and the rivers surged through the city of Winnipeg, the river banks couldn't contain all the extra run-off. So flood waters flowed over low-lying areas. People scrambled to build dikes to stop the rising waters from destroying nearby homes and businesses.

Harry wished his parents could be there that night to help.

But his dad was away at work on the train where he was a porter. His job meant that he was often away for a whole week at a time. And his mother wasn't feeling well these days. Although no one had actually told him, Harry knew there was a baby on the way. For some reason, that was making his mom feel so sick she had to spend most of the time in bed.

"When I'm not here, you have to be the man around the house," his dad had told him before leaving for his shift. "Look after your mom and your sisters."

"Come on, guys," Akela shouted. "Hurry. We got to hurry." The cub master was frantically shoveling sand into the bag Tommy was holding open.

As soon as it was full, Harry grabbed it and dragged it off across the road. This was what—maybe his fiftieth trip? He'd lost count a long time ago. When he heaved the bag up to the soldier beside the dike, he saw even more water was seeping through between the sandbags now. As well, the river was splashing over the wall they'd been trying to build.

"Oh, no you don't," the soldier grunted. He snatched up a board from the side of the road and started throwing dirt and rocks from the ground up onto the dike, trying to patch up the leaks.

Harry grabbed some rocks with his bare hands and tried to

shove them into the wall of the dike as well. But the river splashed over the sandbags even more.

"Kid! Stand back!" the soldier yelled at him. "The dike. It's not going to hold. It's giving wa-aay." His voice cracked as he jumped back.

It was no use. They couldn't stop the water. The river was too fierce. Too violent. Too strong.

In a sudden gush, it forced its way over the dike. The wall of sandbags they'd just built collapsed. Water poured over the damaged dike and streamed onto the road. It rushed toward Harry like a runaway bull.

He sprinted away from it, across the road, and tried to scramble up the pile of sand they'd been digging. Tommy grabbed his hand and hauled him to the top.

"Thanks, Tom," he panted as other kids, their fathers, and mothers milled around him, yelling, trying to escape the rushing torrent.

Over the pandemonium, a siren screamed. The overflowing river surged closer and closer to their sand pile.

The worst thing they could imagine had happened. The Red River had breached its banks. Their dikes had failed.

The fierce river was flooding the city. They'd lost the race.

CHAPTER 2

Over the shrieking siren and shouting people, Harry heard a piercing whistle. Two long, one short. Akela, their cub master. It was the signal that meant all the cub scouts had to come to him. Immediately.

Harry couldn't see him. So many people were rushing around, yelling, grabbing each other, pulling each other up the sand piles to escape from the rising water.

"Come on," Harry yelled at Tommy.

"But my cap. I lost my cap!" Tommy was wildly looking around.

There was the whistle again.

"Forget it," Harry yelled. "We have to find Akela."

"There he is." Tommy pointed. Akela was behind them, in the park. He'd climbed onto a park bench. Water was churning around its feet. Four or five cubs were up on the bench beside him, hanging onto the back railing.

Harry followed Tommy, sliding down the pile of sand and splashing through the streaming water to the park bench.

There wasn't room on the bench, so they stood with some other cubs on some rocks behind it. The water gurgled around their boots, almost over the tops.

"Listen up, fellows," Akela had to raise his voice to be heard over the siren and the shouting mob. "First, thanks for coming out. And for all your hard work. But we can't help here any longer. What I want you all to do is this. Go straight home. Turn on your radio. Listen for the news. If they can't stop the river flooding, the city might have to evacuate."

"Evacuate?" Tommy asked. "What's that?"

"If the water gets any higher, we might have to leave our homes. You could be in danger."

"But where will we go?"

"They'll tell you. The army's here. And the Red Cross. They'll tell us all where to go. Now, straight home. Everyone."

The water around Harry's boots was swirling even higher. He and Tommy splashed across the little park and up to Enfield Crescent. The river hadn't reached the Crescent, but Harry knew that behind them, it was rising steadily.

When they got to their block on Enfield, the houses were far enough away from the river that they weren't under water—yet. A steadily growing torrent was streaming down the street, carrying twigs and other debris. The boys came to Tommy's house first; then Harry carried on alone. It was so windy he had to hang onto his hat so it wouldn't blow away.

When he got home, the whole house was in darkness. At least the back door wasn't locked. His sisters had gone to bed. He peeked into the bedroom the three of them shared and saw them both fast asleep in the double bed. His bed was a narrow one under the window but he didn't go there yet.

He thought his mom was probably asleep as well. Should he tell her he was back home? Maybe not. She'd just get mad at him for waking her.

The cub master had told them to listen to the radio. They had a small one on the kitchen counter but it wasn't working the last time Harry tried it. He turned it on. All he could hear was hissing static. He played with the dial. Nothing. There was another radio in the living room but it was part of his dad's record player console that the kids weren't allowed to use.

Above the sound of icy rain battering the kitchen window, Harry could still hear that siren. What was that about? Couldn't be a fire. Surely no house could be burning down in all this rain.

He was so exhausted now he didn't have the energy to even take off his clothes and go to bed. He collapsed onto a kitchen chair and shook off his boots. His socks were soaked and his toes were numb. He was about to tug off his socks, when there was a loud pounding at the front door.

Must be a stranger. No one ever came to their front door, except the mailman.

Harry ran to answer it.

It was a tall soldier.

"Where are your parents, sonny?" the man asked.

"Um … my mom's sleeping and Dad's away at work."

"Didn't you hear the evacuation notice on the radio?"

Harry shook his head. "Our radio's broken …"

"Look, kid. Everyone has to leave. Right now. Your whole family. The river's gone through another major dike. Won't be long before your street will be under water."

"But … but …"

Before Harry could ask the soldier where they should go, he'd already left and was banging on the neighbor's door.

"Val! Carolyn!" Harry shouted, hurrying to their bedroom, waking his sisters. "We got to leave now! The river's flooding."

"What? Oh, no …" Carolyn cried. "We're all going to die."

"Don't be a dolt," Harry said. "Just get dressed. I'll wake up Mom."

How his mom could sleep through all the screeching sirens and shouting was a mystery. Harry flicked on the overhead light in the bedroom.

"Mom! Mom!" He shook her shoulder.

Finally, she was awake. "Um … what is it?" she muttered.

"The river's flooding. We've got to leave now. Right now. A soldier said."

Harry's mom blinked up at him as if she didn't even recognize him.

"Come on, Mom." He pulled at her arm. "Get your coat on. We need to leave right now. The river. It's flooding."

"Flood? No, no." She stared out the window. "It can't be."

"Here are your shoes, Mom. You got to get dressed."

Another loud banging at the front door. Harry rushed to answer it. He saw his sisters in the hallway. They were already dressed, even had their coats and hats on, and Valerie was clutching her teddy bear. Their eyes were huge with fear and apprehension.

The banging at the door continued. Harry pulled it open. A blast of wind hit his face.

"Good," Mrs. Ball, their neighbor, said. "I'm glad you're awake, Harry. Now where are your parents?"

"Dad's at work …" Harry started.

Behind Mrs. Ball, bare tree branches swayed wildly in the wind. In the beam of light from the streetlight, Harry could see slanted rain mixed with snow. People were rushing up the road, away from the river. They were bundled in scarves and hats. A few struggled with umbrellas, trying to keep them steady in the driving wind. Not many cars in this part of the city.

The siren was still wailing away.

"Mrs. Ball," Harry's mom said to the neighbor. "Hello." She was fully awake now and dressed, buttoning up her long wooly coat, tucking her hair into a scarf. "What a miserable night. What's happening out there?" She was like her old self, all business and energy.

"Ah, Madame Jerome. We must evacuate immediately. The flood, it's putting us all in extreme danger. There's a bus up the hill near Laurentian Street."

"But where are we going?"

"They'll take us all to a safe place until they get the river under control. The army, it's here."

"Come on, kids." Harry's mom got the front door key. "Let's go."

Harry pulled his wet coat and boots back on. His mom locked the door and herded the three of them down the front steps and onto the sidewalk where they joined the crowd hurrying away from the river.

Harry remembered again that his father had told him to look after his sisters and mother while he was away at work. But he was relieved to see his mother was taking charge. That meant she was feeling better. Maybe now she wouldn't be so sick she had to lie down in her darkened bedroom most of the time.

The bus was an old school bus. When they climbed up into it, Harry's mom sighed heavily as she looked around for a vacant seat, but every one was already taken. She stared directly at a snoozing teenager and sighed heavily again. Louder this time. The woman beside the boy prodded his arm until he got up to give Harry's mom his seat.

The boy scowled at Harry, as if it was Harry's fault. Harry turned away and nudged his sisters further back. They pushed their way down the aisle where they stood pressed against other people who couldn't find seats.

The bus's motor started up and, grinding away, it belched smoke they could smell from inside. Harry had to cling to the back of a seat as the bus swayed from side to side, its tires splashing through deep puddles. He tried to see out the steamed-up windows. He had no idea where they were heading.

CHAPTER 3

It looked as if the bus driver wasn't sure where he was going, either, on this dark, wet night. The bus wandered along poorly lit streets, picking up more stranded passengers along the way until there was hardly room to breathe. The bus came to a dead end and the driver had to back it up the whole way. Harry thought they even crossed over the river on a bridge at least once, but he couldn't see much out the fogged-up windows.

All of a sudden, the bus lurched over a big bump and its motor coughed. People squealed as the bus swayed and tilted. Harry had to hold on tight or he would have fallen into the lap of a woman sitting close to him. Water sprayed up to the windows as the bus came to a sputtering stop. Above the passengers' shouting, he could hear the motor grinding away as the bus driver tried to get it running again. No luck.

Where were they now? Did the driver even know? Were they lost?

Lights from outside flashed on the front windshield.

The driver slid open his side window and talked to someone outside. Harry couldn't hear what they were saying, but the driver seemed to be arguing with a man standing right beside the bus.

Finally the driver shook his head and stood, holding up his hands. "Your attention, please, everyone. Your attention." It took a while, but eventually the passengers were quiet enough to hear him. "Sorry about this, folks, but we can't go any further along this street. It's already flooded and I've just been told that the bridge we were heading for has been swept away by the river."

"Oh, no!" A woman standing beside the bus driver buried her face in her hands. "What are we going to do?"

The driver shook his head. "Don't really know what we can do at this point, ma'am. Probably we should all hang on and wait here until the army comes to help us out. They'll be along eventually."

The woman in the seat near Harry wiped the window so now he could see outside. There was water everywhere, streaming down the edge of the road. They had stopped next to a building with a blinking neon sign: Regent Hotel Café.

Now he knew exactly where they were. It wasn't far from Union Station where his dad went to work. Harry had gone with him a few times to help him carry stuff he needed for his job. And once they'd stopped at the cafe and shared a milkshake. Strawberry. Just thinking about that delicious milkshake made him long for his dad. He should be here now. When they needed him.

The CN station was built on slightly higher ground than the surrounding area. And so were the railway tracks. So maybe they'd be safe from the river's rising waters and wouldn't be flooded yet.

Also, Harry remembered that right near the train station, there was a railroad bridge that crossed the Red River. If it hadn't been swept away by the flooding river, wouldn't it carry a train out of town and away from the flood?

He should tell the bus driver about the train station. But he couldn't get the words out. The driver probably wouldn't listen to him, anyway. He was just a kid. No one ever listens to kids.

Everyone around him was talking really loud now, staring at each other with scared faces. Some people looked as if they were gathering up their stuff and getting ready to leave the bus, to head out into the night on their own.

Harry pushed past the other passengers until he was standing behind his mom's seat. He plucked her sleeve. "Um … Mom?"

She turned from the woman she was talking to. "What is it, Harry?"

"We're close to Union Station. You know? Where Dad goes to work."

"Are we?" She shook her head. "It's so dark and wet out there, I really can't tell where we are."

"Maybe the trains are still running. And there's that railway bridge across the river. Maybe the trains are using that to get people out of town. Away from the flood. If we could maybe get on one of those trains …"

"Good idea, Harry …"

She was interrupted by the driver who stood up again, and again asked for everyone's attention. When everyone was quiet, he said, "All right, folks. Here's a question. Does anyone know where we are?"

Harry's mother nodded at Harry to go and tell the driver that he did. When Harry hesitated, she pulled herself up out of her seat and went to talk to him herself. Harry saw him nod and his mom motioned to Harry to come forward.

"Your mother says you might know the way to the train station from here, son?"

Harry nodded. "I've come here with my dad. It's not far. Five minute walk, maybe."

"Think you could show us the way?"

"I … I think so." Harry's stomach was churning. Maybe he'd get them even *more* lost out there in the dark wet night.

But the driver said, "Sounds like our best bet."

He clapped his hands to get everyone's attention again. "All right. Listen up, ladies and gents.

"New plan, folks. We don't know when the army's going to show up here, so we're going to try heading to the train station. This kid says it's not far. We'll have to walk, though. This bus isn't going anywhere tonight."

"Sure hope that kid knows where he's going," Harry heard one man mutter to another behind him.

Harry hoped he did as well.

The passengers grumbled but they started getting ready to leave.

The bus door swished open and Harry was the first to get off. The cold wet wind caught him in the face. He pulled his wooly hat down over his ears. The road was a churning, ankle-deep lake. Good thing he had his rubber boots on.

His sisters and his mom were right behind him. He led them and the rest of the passengers out into the dark night through the pelting rain. They slogged past cars abandoned along the road, then along a back alley he remembered taking with his dad.

A shortcut, his dad had told him. It was even darker here so it was hard to tell for sure if this was the right alley. If it wasn't, he was going to be in a pack of trouble.

He led everyone down the alley, then up a slope until he saw it right in front of them. Union Station. Thank goodness he'd remembered the way.

Yellow light poured out of the doors and windows of the big stone building. The words *Union Station* were carved into the stone facing above the huge curved-top glass front doors.

People from the bus pushed through the doors after him, saying, "Hey, thanks, kid. Thank you …" Soon they disappeared into the crowd.

The station was a massive building with a high round dome in the ceiling, but it was crowded. People of all ages stood around in groups. There was a low rumble as they talked quietly, looking tired and worried, frowning at each other. A small baby was crying, his mother trying to comfort him.

Harry, his sisters, and his mom were crowded up against a wall under a high window. There was nowhere to sit except on the marble floor. But it was muddy and wet.

"Whatever we do, kids," Harry's mom told him and his sisters, "we have to stick together."

It wasn't long before Harry heard a whistle as a train chugged into the station.

"I don't know where that train's heading, but we're going to be on it," Harry's mom said.

"But we don't have tickets," Harry said.

"I'm sure they won't be asking for tickets tonight." She herded him and his sisters toward the embarking gate, pushing them ahead of herself, through the crowd.

It looked as if everyone else had the same idea. The crowd surged toward the train, and Harry and his family had to shove their way through it.

Harry's mom turned back. "Harry. Hold Valerie's hand so she doesn't get lost."

Valerie tried to squirm away but Harry clung onto her wrist and dragged her along.

"My teddy," she whimpered. "My teddy's gone."

"Your teddy doesn't matter now, Val. We've got to get on that train. It might be our only chance to get out of the city tonight."

Harry saw his sister's lip quiver. Usually Valerie was really tough. She never cried about anything. He saw his mom and Carolyn pushing themselves ahead through the crowd and climbing the steps onto the train. Beside him, Valerie sniffed and rubbed her nose on the back of her hand.

"Okay, where'd you leave your stupid teddy? Did you leave it on the bus?"

"No. I had him. Just a minute ago ..." Harry could see that his sister was trying hard not to cry.

His mother and Carolyn had disappeared into the train now. It took him only a second to decide. "Fine. We'll go back to where we were standing. Maybe it's there."

He sprinted back. Sure enough, there it was. Someone had found it and propped it up on the high window ledge.

Harry had to jump to reach it. It was all muddy on one side. He tried to brush it off, then threw it at Valerie. She caught it and smiled, hugging it close, the mud smearing her cheek.

"Come on now. We can't miss that train."

The crowd was even thicker now and more anxious. Parents shouted out and, clinging to their frightened children, shouldered their way toward the train.

Pulling Valerie behind him, Harry ducked under elbows and slithered past feet until they were at the tracks.

"All aboard!" he heard the conductor shout above all the commotion. "All aboard!"

The train started to move. No! They'd missed it.

A doorway appeared. It was still open.

"Grab on," Harry grunted as he shoved his sister with his shoulder onto the steps. She grabbed the metal railing and hung on.

"Harry!" She reached out to him as he sprinted alongside the moving train.

At the last minute, he caught the railing and swung himself up after her. They scrambled up the steps and into the train car. Harry was panting hard. He stopped to catch his breath and look around. The car was packed. Every seat was taken. Even big kids were sitting on their parents' laps. The aisles were jammed with people standing, eyeing the seated people with envy.

But at least he and his sister were on the train. They'd made it.

"Where's Mom and Carolyn?" Valerie asked, her eyes searching the crowded car. There was no sign of their mother or sister.

"They must be in another car," Harry said. "Come on. We'll find them."

He threaded his way through the crowd, lurching from car to car, pulling Valerie along. They passed a conductor helping passengers stuff their bundles onto over-crowded storage racks.

Harry worried for a moment that the conductor was going ask them for their tickets but he just nodded at them as Harry slipped past with Valerie in tow.

He finally found their mother sitting in one of the cars near the front of the train. Carolyn was perched on her lap.

"There you are." Their mother hugged them both. "I was so worried you two were lost. Now didn't I tell you to stick with me ..." she scolded.

Harry glanced over her shoulder to Valerie who squeezed her teddy close and sucked in her lips to keep from smiling at him.

He might not be a real superhero, he thought, but tonight, maybe his sister might think so ...

CHAPTER 4

The train trundled across the river on the train bridge, hooting its whistle, the sound echoing off the dark water swirling below. A wave of exhaustion washed over Harry. He was so tired, his legs were wobbly and wouldn't hold him upright. His mom was sitting in the last seat in the car so there was a small space behind her. He slumped down into the space and curled up on the floor. His head sunk to his arms and he dozed off.

"Harry. Harry. Wake up." His mother was shaking his shoulder.

He opened his eyes and saw a faint light trickling in the train windows, clouded by mist and rain. Was it morning? Where were they?

"We're getting out at the next stop," his mother said. She stood up and held Carolyn with one hand and Valerie with the other. She nodded to Harry to follow them.

They stayed in a small town outside of Winnipeg with several other families in a church hall for a long boring week. Harry had no idea what town it was or even how far away it was from St. Boniface.

They slept on musty-smelling gym mats and ate food prepared in big pots by the local women in the town. During the day, Harry's sisters played with their cut-outs from Eaton's catalogs with some other girls, creating whole pretend worlds.

In the meantime, Harry found a bunch of boys who liked baseball as much as he did. So when they could find a bat and ball, and when it wasn't pouring too hard, they played out in the school's rain-soaked playground across the street.

As the days dragged on, the burst of energy and cheer Harry's mom had had during the night of the evacuation seemed to ebb away. Soon she was spending most of her time napping on a mat she'd set up in a quiet corner of the hall.

After a few days, Harry's father found them and came to visit. He arrived just as the church ladies were serving bowls of hot chicken soup for lunch. Valerie spotted him first.

"Daddy," she squealed and ran to him.

He caught her up in a big hug and swung her around. Harry and Carolyn ran to hug him as well. His long wool coat was scratchy against Harry's cheek and he smelled like a combination of fresh air and smoke from the train. He seemed to have grown even taller and thinner since they'd seen him a couple of weeks before. But his big grin was just as wide and happy. He told them he'd heard their house was still standing. It hadn't been swept away by the rising river. But it had been flooded, all right, as had all the houses on their street.

At the end of a week or so, the weather turned warm and sunny. Harry and his family returned to St. Boniface, again by train. When they got there, they found the river had fallen to a safer level behind the rebuilt sandbag dikes. But it had left behind a gritty mess, including garbage and branches strewn everywhere on the streets and sidewalks and even on the lawns and gardens. The worst part was the horrible smell of damp and rot that seemed to be baking in the sunshine. It was so awful, it made Harry feel like throwing up.

When his mother saw the inside of their house, she burst into tears. Her tidy house was a total disaster. The floors were covered with sand and debris. Even her new curtains in the kitchen were stained and torn.

"Everything is just ruined ..." she wailed.

Harry's boots scrunched down the hallway as he waded through damp rubble to the bedroom he shared with his sisters.

He pushed the door open, scraping it against the gritty floor. Yuck! What a stench! It smelled even worse in there than it did outside. A lot worse. The smell was so disgusting, he had to pull his sweater up over his mouth and nose and hold his breath.

He stepped inside the room. The window above his bed was broken and the windowsill was thick with sandy garbage—including a dead bird, its beak open and its tiny tongue hanging out. Flies were buzzing around it.

His bedding was strewn with broken glass and soaked with muck. When he checked under the bed, he found his hoard of comics. But when he tried to pull one out, it fell apart in his fingers. His whole collection was a soaking-wet mess. Tears prickled his eyes. He wanted to slam the bedroom door and shut out the terrible scene, but his sisters were right behind him.

"What a stink!" Carolyn pushed past him. "Oh, yuck! A dead bird! Daddy! Daddy! There's a dead bird in here …" she yelled, running to the living room. Harry followed her.

Their dad was standing there in the wrecked living room, gazing at their most prized possession—the big shiny wooden combo radio and record player console. He'd spent hours listening to his stack of jazz records on it. Louis Armstrong, Sidney Bechet, Earl Hines, Jelly Roll Morton. Harry knew them all.

His father picked up a record. Its cardboard jacket was so sodden, it disintegrated in his hands and the record tumbled to the floor and shattered. He shook his head and stared down at it.

"Well, kids. This is it. We're going to move. As soon as we can get this house all cleaned and fixed up, we'll sell it and move some place far away from this town."

"But we can't move away," Harry's mom said. "We can't leave all our friends and family. What about my sisters?"

"I've heard that lots of people around here are planning to move," Harry's dad said. "This city should never have been built so close to the river. Every spring it's going to keep on flooding. No reason to think it won't. I've got a hankering to move out west, to British Columbia. Do you know that some years, the winter's so mild there on the west coast, it doesn't even get snow? Now, wouldn't that be great? You'll all love it."

He'd been out west on the train, and he'd heard from his fellow porters that the west coast was a wonderful place to live, to bring up a family. Although the houses in Vancouver might be a bit more expensive, and it might rain a lot sometimes, you could buy a house far away from a river that flooded every spring.

They would sell this house and buy a good place for a family in one of Vancouver's suburbs. Maybe North Vancouver. Since

Vancouver was a major train stop, he could keep his job as a porter on the train. As an Afro-Canadian, it would be hard to find another job as good as that one in Canada in the 1950s.

It took a lot of hard work, shoveling and scrubbing and painting, to get their house ready to sell. Harry and his sisters helped. It was a huge job. They helped pry up the moldy tiles in the kitchen and pile all the rotting furniture and bedding into a big heap in front of the house to be collected by the garbage trucks. They even found another dead bird—this one rotting in the bathtub. The girls refused to have a bath until their mom had scrubbed out the tub with bleach. Even after they'd left the window open for days, Harry thought he could still smell it.

A few months later, Harry's little brother, Barton, was born. He was a fussy baby, crying most of the time, night and day. If his mother was tired before the baby was born, she was even more tired after.

Harry started to spend as much time as he could away from home, and away from the noise of his squalling baby brother and his forever exhausted mom. He and his pal, Tommy Leblanc, played endless games of scrub with their friends after school in the grounds of Queen Elizabeth School or on the street. Harry's favorite part of those games was catching fly balls. He was pretty good at it and loved the satisfying smack they made in his hands. One day, maybe he'd get himself a good glove.

Finally, more than a year later, in the summer of 1951, the day came when the house on Enfield Crescent in St. Boniface was sold and the family was ready to move west. They didn't pack any furniture. Most of it had been ruined by the flood or given away to charity. They crated up their few clothes and bedding. There were no books or toys. Except for Valerie's special bear.

"We can get everything we need once we're settled in Vancouver," Harry's dad told them. He had arranged with a real estate agent in North Vancouver to find them a decent house in a good part of town.

Harry didn't want to move. He'd have to leave his good friend, Tommy. And his cub pack as well.

"You'll be turning eleven soon," his dad told him. "We'll find you a Scout troop in North Vancouver."

CHAPTER 5

The real estate agent found them a good house in North Vancouver, with trees and flowers and a manicured lawn in the front yard. There was a spacious living room and modern kitchen where they even had a telephone. Everything was so fresh and clean and new, it made Harry grin. His sisters sure liked it. They ran from room to room, squealing with delight. Even their mother seemed to like it.

Best of all, the house had three bedrooms so Harry didn't have to share a bedroom with his sisters. His baby brother would be sleeping in their parents' bedroom so they didn't have far to go when he woke up in the night. For now, anyway, Harry had the luxury of a whole room to himself.

Before they'd even unpacked their suitcases and boxes, there was a knock on the front door. Harry went to answer it, thinking it was probably one of the neighbors coming over to welcome them to the neighborhood, which is what his mother would do.

But he was wrong. Without a word or even a smile, a plump woman with wiry hair thrust a large envelope into his hands. She sniffed, then said, "It's for your parents." Turning away, she hurried back down the sidewalk.

"Who was that?" his mother called from the kitchen where she was making spaghetti for supper.

"Don't know. Some woman. She said this was for you and Dad." Harry gave his mom the envelope.

"Wonder what this could be." She tore it open. "I don't understand …" she murmured as she examined the contents. It was several sheets of paper with what looked like people's signatures and addresses.

"Let's see," Harry's dad said. He was sitting at the kitchen table, drinking a cup of tea. He flipped through the first page. "Of all the stupid, ignorant …" He slapped the papers down on the table so hard his tea spilled over them. "Ridiculous! This is absolutely ridiculous." He was so furious his face turned purple.

Harry gulped and drew away. He couldn't remember ever seeing his father so angry.

"What is it?" Harry's mom asked. "I couldn't make it out."

"It's a petition. From the other people who live here," he said between tight, angry lips. "They're saying they don't want us here. They say it's a 'whites only' neighborhood. Who do they think they are, anyway?" He pounded his fist on the table, making the tea cups clatter.

"But they can't do that, can they?" Harry's mom looked as if she was about to burst into tears.

Baby Barton did. He'd been asleep in a carry-cot in a corner of the kitchen. Harry's mom sighed as she went to pick him up. "I thought he'd sleep for at least another hour."

"I'm going to call that real estate fellow and see what he says." Harry's father reached for the phone.

"What's happening?" Carolyn rushed from her bedroom with Valerie.

"Some people have made a petition saying we can't live here. That it's a 'whites only' neighborhood." Their mother had to raise her voice above baby Barton's screams. She rocked him in her arms, trying to get him to stop crying. "They can't do that. Can they, Harry?" she asked Harry's dad. "After all, this is Canada. Not the United States. We can live anywhere we want, can't we?" There were tears in her eyes and she tried to sniff them back.

"What?" Carolyn's voice was shrill over Barton's screams. "Someone says we can't live here? They can't make us move out of our new house, can they? Can they, Daddy?"

"They just did," Harry muttered. His head was so hot and prickly with anger and humiliation, it felt as if it was about to explode.

He'd suspected all along that he wasn't going to like this new town. Now he *knew* he hated Vancouver. Stupid, prejudiced neighbors. How could they be so mean? So ignorant? Didn't they know that he and his family were just as good as they were? Why couldn't they be nice and friendly like people were in St. Boniface?

Harry kicked the leg of the table and glared out the kitchen window at the house next door. Who'd want to live near such mean, narrow-minded people, anyway?

But deep, deep down inside himself, so deep down that no one would ever suspect it was there, was a tiny voice that whispered: Maybe they're right. Maybe their new neighbors were right. Maybe brown people like him and his family shouldn't be allowed to live next to white people.

Maybe they really weren't good enough to live in such a nice house ...

CHAPTER 6

The real estate agent came over the next morning and talked to Harry's father behind the closed door of the living room. Harry's mom stayed in the kitchen, trying to soothe Barton, who'd been especially upset since they'd left St. Boniface. Harry hung around in the hall so he could hear the men's conversation.

"No point trying to change these people's minds," Mr. Chance, the real estate agent, said. "They're bigots. Pure and simple."

"But isn't it against the law to exclude people from a neighborhood because of their race or religion?"

"True. But would you really want to live somewhere that was so unfriendly? Just think of your family. Your kids. Would they be happy here?"

"You say you can find us another house in a friendlier part of North Vancouver?"

"Right. I've got a listing for another good house. A bit smaller, but it would be cheaper. And it's right on the bus line."

After a long talk with the real estate agent, Harry's father agreed to look at the new house in what seemed a friendlier part of town.

As the real estate agent had said, the house was smaller. It was older, too, and shabbier. The kitchen had an old chipped electric stove and fridge, but Harry still had his own bedroom. It was tiny, barely room enough for his bed and a small dresser. But at least he didn't have to share with his sisters.

They would be starting at a new school soon after moving to the new house, right after the summer holidays. Harry would be in Grade 6, Carolyn in Grade 4, and Valerie in Grade 2.

Their mom probably wouldn't be able go with them on the first day because of the baby. And neither would their dad because he'd be away at work. His shifts on the train where he was a porter usually lasted for a week or even longer when he had to travel all the way to Montreal and back to the west coast, instead of just to Winnipeg and back.

But Harry and his sisters were old enough to start school on their own. All they had to do was show up at the new school with their report cards from their school in St. Boniface to show what grades they were in.

The school wasn't far away—just up the street and over a couple of blocks. On the weekend before leaving for his shift at work, Harry's father took the three of them for a walk up the hill so they could see what the new school looked like.

"Your first day of school is on Tuesday after Labor Day," he said to them in his "this-is-very-important" voice. "Now remember. The most valuable thing you children can do, is get a good education. The best education you can. I don't want you to be stuck in a dead-end job like mine for your whole life. Being a porter is fine for now, but with a good education, you'll be able to do anything you want. A good education is the key to a better life."

He went on talking about how he hadn't had the chance to finish school because he'd had to go to work to help support his father and mother and the rest of the family when he was still a teenager.

Harry was half listening to him as he watched a bunch of kids playing baseball in the school playground. This new school was just one story high and it looked a lot more modern than Queen Elizabeth School on Enfield Crescent he and his sisters had attended in St. Boniface.

The kids looked around his age. They were having fun, shouting and cheering each other along. He wished he had enough nerve to go up to them and ask if he could play baseball, too. But they'd probably say no. Maybe some of them were even from the same part of town where he and his family had been kicked out when they first moved to North Vancouver. The "whites only" neighborhood.

"All right," he told his dad. "We know where we have to come on Tuesday. Can we go home now?"

Along with the night of the flood in St. Boniface the year before, that first day of school was a day that would be carved into Harry's memory for as long as he lived.

After a quick breakfast of bread and peanut butter, Harry was ready to leave for school. Before leaving for his work shift on the train a couple of days before, his father had told him, as usual, to look after his sisters.

"Come on," Harry urged Carolyn and Valerie. "We don't want to be late on our first day."

"But I can't find my report card," Carolyn moaned.

"Look." Valerie pointed out. "It's right here on the counter where Mom left it."

Harry huffed impatiently and headed for the back door, shoving his own report card into the back pocket in his pants.

"Wait for me," Carolyn squealed. "I've got to finish my hair." She was trying to tie her curly hair back into a ponytail, but the ribbon kept slipping away.

"Here," Valerie said. "You hold your hair and I'll do it." She tied the ribbon in a quick bow.

"Be quiet, you dolts," Harry hissed their way. "You're going to wake Mom."

Their mom still wasn't up when they left. Harry had heard their baby brother crying in the night, but now both he and their mom were asleep. Although Barton was over a year old now, he still usually didn't sleep through the night. Harry knew better than to try to wake them.

He remembered with a pang when things were different a couple of years ago. That was before Barton was born. Their mom would always be up to give him and his sisters breakfast. Sometimes she would even walk them to school.

"I should have brought my coat." Carolyn crossed her arms as she followed Harry outside. She shivered against the wind and looked up at the cloudy sky.

"It's not that cold," Harry said. "Besides, we'll be inside the school most of the day, anyway."

"Hope I get a nice teacher," Valerie said.

Of the three of them, she was the only one who actually *liked* school.

It had rained in the night and there were lots of puddles on the road up the hill on their way to school. Harry made sure to step over them. His right shoe had a hole in the sole and he didn't want to spend all day at school wearing a wet sock.

When they got to school, some kids were still outside playing in the playground. That meant the bell hadn't rung yet.

Some of the kids were playing baseball. Was it the same bunch they had seen a few days ago? Harry wondered as he stood with his sisters beside the row of trees at the edge of the field. They watched the kids throw and hit the ball.

The air smelled good here. Fresh and spicy from the evergreen trees.

Harry longed with all his heart to join the game. It would be so much fun to wallop the ball and race around the bases.

A boy swung the bat and hit the ball with a loud crack. It was a high one, a fly ball. It flew toward Harry. He sprinted out, got under it, and caught it. Smack. The ball stung his bare hands.

"You're out," a kid yelled.

"What d'you mean 'out'? That kid wasn't even playing," the batter yelled back. "Hey—he's a coolie. Don'tcha even know that dumb coolies aren't allowed to play," he yelled at Harry.

What had that kid called him? A coolie? A dumb coolie? By the way the boy had curled his lip and scrunched up his nose when he said "coolie," Harry knew he'd meant it as an insult. But he was so surprised to be yelled at like that, for a second, he couldn't move. Coolie? What did that mean, anyway? No one had ever called him that before.

He stood there, holding the baseball as if he were paralyzed. His palms were still stinging. He didn't know what to do with the ball.

"Hey, kid," the pitcher yelled at him. "Give us back our ball."

Harry shrugged. He pegged the ball right at the pitcher. Hard. It hit the boy in the stomach.

"Oof …" the pitcher muttered as he doubled over in pain.

A short kid with a brush-cut picked up a rock.

"You get away, kid," he yelled at Harry. "We don't want no dumb rotten coolies round here. No stupid coolies allowed." He threw the rock, hitting Harry in the arm.

Harry's arm smarted. And his head throbbed with anger. He picked up an even bigger rock and hurled it back. Someone yelled out in pain. Harry didn't care. Those mean kids were the ones who'd started the fight. He ducked and another rock just missed his head.

He was going to throw another rock, but Valerie pulled his sleeve. "Come on, Harry," she squeaked. "Come on. Let's go. We got to get out of here."

Before he could even turn around, a bunch of other kids ran toward them, pelting them with rocks, calling them names, yelling at them to go home. It seemed as if every kid in the playground was throwing rocks and yelling at them now.

Carolyn cried out as a rock hit her shoulder.

"Okay. Come on. Let's go," Harry said as more kids advanced on them, faces distorted with anger and chanting, "Coolies! Stupid coolies! Get lost, you dirty coolies ..."

He sprinted down the hill toward home. Glancing back, he saw his sisters were running right behind him, their faces bunched up with fear.

When they got to their house, he hesitated before going inside. What was he going to tell their mom? He couldn't tell her they'd been in a fight at school. She'd be so mad at them for getting into a fight. Even if it hadn't been their fault.

His sisters caught up with him in the front yard. They were both breathless.

"Why are those kids so mean?" Carolyn cried, panting, trying to catch her breath. Her face was red and her eyes filled with tears.

"Because they're ignorant and stupid," Harry said, trying to swallow his anger and keep his voice calm. "Anyway, whatever we do, we can't tell Mom."

"Why not?" Valerie asked, ducking under the eaves at the side of the house to shelter from the rain.

"She'll just get mad and blame us for getting into a fight."

It had started to rain, just a sprinkle. But if they stayed outside, they'd soon be soaked.

"Mom's probably still sleeping, anyways," Carolyn said, sniffing back her tears.

Harry nodded. "If we go in and we're really quiet, we won't wake her."

So they went around to the back door and crept into the house and through the kitchen. Harry snuck down the hall, past his parents' bedroom to his own room. There, he flung himself onto his bed without even taking off his shoes.

His head pounded with anger. He felt like crying but he squeezed his eyes shut and wouldn't let himself. What a crappy place to live, he thought. No way was he ever going back to that stupid school.

He reached under his bed to his stash of comics and pulled out a couple from the top. *Classics Illustrated*. He still liked superhero comics but now the Classics were right up there among his favorites. The top comic on the pile was *The Battles of Thor, Norse God of Thunder*.

Harry stared at the cover. Thor's muscles bulged as he swung his mystical hammer called Mjolnir above his head. He could defeat any enemy in battle with his stupendous strength and his mystical hammer.

That's what Harry needed. A mystical hammer. He'd use it to bash off the heads of all those ugly jerks who had thrown rocks at him and his sisters and called them nasty names. That would fix them.

Anyways, there's no way he was going back to that stinking, rotten, bag of puke school, ever.

CHAPTER 7

A couple of hours later, Harry was still reading comics in his bedroom. He heard his mom. "What are you girls doing home?" Her voice was scratchy, as if she had a bad cold.

"Lunch." That was Carolyn's voice.

"Is Harry here, too?"

No point hiding out in his room.

"Yeah, I'm here," he said, coming into the kitchen.

"Open a can of soup for lunch, will you, Harry?" his mom asked him, putting on the kettle for tea. She had dark smudges under her eyes and her long hair was sticking out all over her head. She was still in her dressing gown and she smelled like sour milk. "Just be quiet. Whatever you do, don't wake up that baby. He was up again all night and I didn't get a wink of sleep."

After they'd each had a bowl of vegetable soup and some soda crackers, they left. They couldn't hang around the house or their mom would start asking about why they weren't in school.

"Where are we going?" Carolyn asked on their way out.

"Don't know," Harry mumbled as he headed back up the hill. "But not back to that stinking, rotten school, that's for darn sure." It was raining harder now so he pulled his jacket closer around his neck.

When they turned the corner, he noticed a green wooden shack in the lane. There was a sign above the door that read: *The Vancouver Sun*. And the door was open.

Harry climbed the three steps to the door and peered inside. No one was there. And it was dry.

"We could wait in here. At least until it stops raining."

His sisters followed him inside. The shack was empty except for a few old newspapers on the floor and a cardboard box in the corner, overflowing with bits of thin wire and string.

"I don't think we're supposed to be here." Valerie glanced around anxiously. "Shouldn't we try going back to school?"

"You can wait out in the rain for all I care," Harry told her. "Or go back to that stupid school. But you'll never catch me going there. Never in a million years."

Valerie stared at the door as if she was trying to make up her mind whether to leave or not.

"At least it's dry in here." Carolyn was making herself comfortable on a bench beside a pile of crumpled newspapers. "So now what are we going to do?" she asked Harry.

"Search me," he grunted, picking up a crumpled newspaper. Smoothing it out, he saw it was the sports section and there were articles about the baseball games leading up to the World Series. The New York Yankees vs. the New York Giants. One article was about a promising young rookie player named Willie Mays and a photo of him with a caption reading: *Rookie kid from Westfield, Alabama. Is he the slam hitter the Giants need to win the Series?*

Harry stared at the photo. The baseball player looked a lot like him with his dark eyes, curly hair, and brown skin. That's what he should do. He should learn to hit baseballs really hard, and become a star baseball player. Then no one would ever dare call him a stupid coolie. Or anything else.

Valerie picked up some string from the box in the corner and made a loop with it. She and Carolyn played cat's cradle, making different designs with the string.

After an hour or so, Harry heard a van back up just outside the shack.

"Uh-oh," Carolyn said. "Now what?"

Harry peered out the door and saw that the back of the van

was open, and it was full of stacks of newspapers.

A man climbed out of the passenger's side of the van and started walking toward the shack.

Oh, no! They were caught. Where could they hide?

"Hey, kid," the man said. "Glad you're early. Don't just stand there. Give us a hand unloading, will ya?"

He was a tall man. At least as tall as Harry's dad. He was wearing a baseball cap and chewing a toothpick.

It was still raining, but Harry jumped from the doorway of the shack to the ground and grabbed the bundle of newspapers the man unloaded from the back. Harry wasn't sure where to put them. Probably inside the shack. They'd stay dry there.

Carolyn appeared in the doorway. He tossed the bundle up to her. "Just pile them inside," he told her.

"See you brought along your help," the man said.

"My sister." Harry grabbed another bundle of newspapers and handed it up to Carolyn to stack inside.

"So where's your shack supervisor? He should be here by now. He's got to sort out the papers into the different routes."

"Maybe he's still at school …?" Harry said.

"Right. First day of school today. You can get the sorting started. Here's our list for today."

The man handed Harry a typed page. Down the side of the page was a row of the letters of the alphabet with various numbers beside each one. Like, beside A, there was 38. Beside B, there was 52, and so on.

"Ah …" Harry didn't want to admit that he had no idea what the guy was talking about.

"You just count out the number of newspapers, put them in piles, and write the letter on the top paper. Got it?"

"Oh, right." That sounded pretty easy.

"Here. I'll cut those bailing wires for you so you can get started counting." The man pulled a cutting device from his pocket and snapped the wires open. "That's it. Got to go. Tell Rob to give me a call tonight if he can't get here every day by 2:45. I'll have to find someone else to do his job. We have to have the papers all ready for when the carriers arrive here after school to deliver them. One thing people hate is waiting for their newspapers."

Job. When Harry heard that word, his heart jumped. He wanted a job more than anything. Money was so tight at home these days that sometimes his dad didn't have enough left over, after paying for food and the mortgage on the house, to give Harry and his sisters their weekly allowance of twenty-five cents each. That meant that some weeks they couldn't buy themselves any treats at all, not even a comic book or a package of gum.

Before Harry had a chance to ask about getting a job, the tall man had jumped back into the truck and taken off.

"Hey, you guys want to help?" he asked his sisters.

Soon they had all the stacks of newspaper piled up in neat rows on the wooden bench inside the shack. Valerie even found the stub of a pencil in her pocket so Harry could write the right letters on each stack. They were just finishing the last pile when a harried teenager arrived on his bike. He skidded to a stop in front of the shack. He was puffing hard, trying to catch his breath.

He looked surprised to see Harry and his sisters in there but he didn't chase them away. He was even more surprised when he saw the tidy rows of stacks of newspapers inside the shack. "What's happening?" He scratched his head.

"Are you Rob?" Harry asked.

"Yeah."

"The delivery guy asked us to sort out the papers. He said for you to call him on the phone tonight if you can't be here by 2:45 every day."

The teenager nodded. "I can get here most days. Just today being the first day at school, I got sort of delayed, you know?"

"Right. Say, do you need any more paperboys? I could do it." Harry held his breath and waited while the guy scratched his head again and stared at him.

"You're pretty small. You know you have to be at least eleven to have a route. You're not eleven, are you?"

"Sure am," Harry lied, standing up his tallest and puffing out his chest. He wouldn't actually turn eleven until the end of the month. He stared at his sisters with his mouth pressed shut, willing them not to say anything.

Valerie, especially, had this thing about always telling the truth. Thank goodness she didn't blurt out that Harry was still only ten.

"One kid, name's Steve, he's moving away next week. He has route D, I think. Let's see." Rob looked at the paper with all the letters and numbers on it. "Pretty small route. Only thirty-two papers. You get one cent a paper, so your pay would be just thirty-two cents a day."

"Thirty-two cents *every* day!" Harry felt like jumping up to the moon. "I'd *love* to do it."

"Okay. I'll tell Steve when he gets here. You could shadow him today and learn the route, then take over next week. I'll get an application for you to fill in and have your parents sign."

Harry felt like he'd just won the Irish Sweepstakes. Thirty-two cents a day. He was going to be rich!

"One good thing about getting a paper route with the *Sun* is they've got this great program that, if you keep the route for at least two years, you can get a scholarship to go to university when you finish high school," Rob told him. "That's what I'm doing next year."

"Sounds good," Harry nodded. He couldn't stop himself from smiling at the teenager. This guy was being so nice. Maybe not everyone in North Vancouver was an ignorant bigot.

And, boy! Would his dad ever be impressed! Harry had never heard of anyone in their family, ever, who'd gone to university.

But that meant he'd have to finish high school.

Unfortunately, he'd already quit elementary school, and he was just going into Grade 6.

CHAPTER 8

"I think we should be going to school," Valerie said a couple of mornings later.

"You can go if you want," said Harry. "But I'm not going back to that stupid school. Those jerks will gang up on us again, for sure. Besides, it's past nine o'clock so school will already be started."

"What are you going to do all day, then?"

"Wait at the newspaper shack again, I guess." He was loading a stack of comics into a paper grocery bag. At least he'd have them to read while he waited for the newspapers to be delivered to the shack. "I told Rob I'd sort out the papers for him again if he wasn't there on time."

As usual, their mother wasn't up. She seemed to be in bed a lot of the time these days, except when she had to get up to feed the baby or make herself a cup of tea. So she didn't know that they were spending the day at the newspaper shack and not going to school.

Life was so different for Harry and his sisters since their baby brother had come along. Maybe once Barton was older and sleeping through the night, their mom could get a good night's rest and she'd be back to being her old busy self again.

Harry grabbed his jacket off the hook by the door and was about to leave when he heard someone coming up the back steps.

"Dad!" Valerie and Carolyn squealed and raced to hug him.

"I thought you weren't getting home until the weekend," Harry said, kicking his bag of comics under the table.

"Got the short shift just to Winnipeg and back this time. So what's up?" Without taking off his overcoat and fedora hat, he put his small suitcase on the floor beside the table.

"Not much." Harry was super uncomfortable. He thought he'd have more time to think up some excuse to tell his dad about why they weren't in school.

"I'm surprised to see you three still here. It's almost ten o'clock and it's a school day. Why aren't you all in school?"

"Well ... um ... here's the thing, Dad." Harry shuffled uneasily under his father's searching gaze. "We tried to go to school on Tuesday but they wouldn't let us in."

"Wouldn't let you in? What are you talking about?"

"That's right, Daddy," Carolyn said. "We tried going. Really we did."

"We had our report cards ready and everything," Valerie added.

"So? What happened? Who wouldn't let you in?" Harry's dad put his hands on his hips and stared straight at his son, his dark eyes serious and his eyebrows frowning.

Harry remembered that before leaving for his shift, his dad had told him, as usual, to look after his sisters. And he'd done that. Right?

"When we got to the school grounds, the kids there all ganged up on us."

"They called us names," Valerie piped up. "Not very nice names."

"And they threw rocks at us. A whole bunch of rocks. One hit me on my back. See?" Carolyn pulled her sweater off her shoulder to show him. "I've still got a bruise right here."

Harry nodded. "They started beating us up and they chased us away and … and …"

It wasn't often that Harry saw his father get mad. But he sure was furious now. Even angrier than a few weeks ago when that woman arrived with the petition that said they'd have to move.

"You girls get your coats on," Harry's dad said through angry lips. "And get your report cards. We're going to settle this matter. Right now."

"But, Dad," Harry said, patting his jeans pocket for his report card. "They don't want us at that school. They said we weren't allowed there. Just like they didn't want us in that other neighborhood."

"You three have just as much right to attend that school as any other kid. Come on. Let's go."

Taking long, angry strides, he marched the three of them up the hill, past the newspaper shack, and along the block, his overcoat billowing out behind him.

Harry had to jog to keep up. His sisters ran behind them, panting like worn-out puppies.

When they got to the school, the playground was empty. Of course. The bell had rung ages ago and all the kids would be inside their classrooms.

Without a word, Harry's dad flung open the school's front door and ushered his kids inside. Harry dragged his feet.

Beside the entrance was a door with a glass window. The word OFFICE was printed in black letters on it. Harry's dad pushed that door open and nodded for the kids to go inside.

There was another door with a sign in black letters that said PRINCIPAL. That door was firmly closed.

Beside it was a high counter. Behind the counter sat a woman at a cluttered desk.

"Yes?" she said in a high, unfriendly voice, glancing up from her typewriter.

"I would like to see the principal," Harry's father said in his deep, rumbly voice, removing his hat. "Now."

"And do you have an appointment?"

"No. But this is an urgent matter." Harry's father looked as if he'd barge into the principal's office whether he was invited or not.

"The principal is very busy now, but I'll check if he has time to see you," the woman said. "Who shall I say is calling?"

"Mr. Harry Jerome," Harry's father said. "Senior."

The woman raised her eyebrows and stared at Harry and his sisters. Her red-lipsticked mouth screwed up as if she was smelling something disgusting, like doggy doo-doo. She knocked on the principal's door and slipped inside.

Another ignorant bigot, Harry thought as he listened hard at the whispering from the room, but he couldn't make out what they were saying.

A few minutes later, the woman came out, shutting the door firmly behind her. She still had on her sour face.

"I'm sorry, the principal isn't able to see you now. But if you'd care to make an appointment and come back …"

"As I said, this is an *urgent* matter. It can't wait." Harry's dad opened the principal's door and pushed the three kids into the office ahead of him.

Yikes, Harry thought. We shouldn't be here. He felt like running away and never coming back. His heart was bouncing around in his chest. He shuffled into the room with his hands in his pockets, wishing he was anywhere but here.

A man with a shiny bald head and a red nose was sitting behind a large desk. He jumped to his feet when Harry and his family entered.

"Didn't my secretary tell you that I can't see you at the moment?" He was a tall man with broad shoulders and had a deep, gravelly voice.

"This won't take long." Harry's father held his hat in front of his chest. His voice was softer, more polite now. But Harry could tell that he was as furious as ever. "There seems to be some kind of problem here. You see, my children came to your school last Tuesday, all set to start the school year here. But they were attacked and driven away by some of your students with rocks and nasty name calling."

"Now, now. I'm sure that nothing of the sort happened. I would certainly have heard about it." The principal pulled out a large handkerchief and blotted his sweating forehead.

"It's true," Carolyn said. "They did throw rocks at us. See? I still have a bruise right here …" She started to pull her sweater off her shoulder to show the principal.

Harry was feeling even more uncomfortable. He remembered that it wasn't only the other kids who had thrown rocks. He'd thrown one himself.

"They called us names," Valerie piped up. Harry was surprised she said anything. She was usually the shyest of them all. "And … and they said we weren't allowed to come to this school."

The principal just stood there, shaking his head, as if he didn't believe a word Harry's sisters said.

"I'm sure you'll find room in your school, immediately, for my three children, sir," Harry's father continued, his voice not so polite or quiet now. "And if I hear that there's any problem, any incidents of name calling or rock throwing, whatsoever, I'll be reporting it directly to the head of the school board."

"Oh, now, I don't think that will be necessary, Mr. Jerome."

The principal smiled the phoniest smile Harry had ever seen. His long white teeth glinted between thin lips. "We'll have your children enrolled into their classes right away. And if any student bothers any of you in any way at all," he said, puffing out his chest and pointing sternly at Harry and his sisters, "you are to come and report directly to me, immediately. Now, is that clear?"

Harry blinked and took a step back.

"What is clear is that I, personally, will not stand," Harry's dad pounded the top of the principal's desk with his large brown fist, "for *anyone* harassing my kids. Any time. Any place. Anywhere. They're here to get an education. A *good* education. Now, is *that* clear?" He shook his fist in front of the principal's face.

The principal looked shocked, and suddenly seemed quite a bit smaller, like a pricked balloon shriveling up.

Harry was so embarrassed by his father's angry outburst, he didn't know where to look. But he was also kind of proud of his father. His father wasn't scared of the tall scary principal one bit.

That day was the first day of school in North Vancouver for the three Jerome kids. In the weeks and months to follow, there wasn't any more rock throwing. But the name calling still happened. Sometimes in whispers, but lots of times in loud taunts. Harry soon found that the best way to stop the teasing was to ignore it and walk away. But sometimes that was hard to do. He knew he could never tell the principal about the taunts and insults thrown at him. There was one thing for sure. He didn't want his father to find out about it. He would do almost anything to avoid another embarrassing confrontation with the principal.

One thing he couldn't wait to tell his father about, though, was his newspaper carrier job. Especially the part about the carriers getting scholarships to go to university. He knew his father was going to love that.

CHAPTER 9

Harry didn't make many friends at school. He was too shy and quiet. He spent most of the time slinking around, his head down, trying to be invisible, trying not to attract attention.

Except when it came to baseball. Harry loved baseball. Every chance he got, he played baseball. Every recess and lunchtime. It was soon clear he was a pretty good ballplayer. He could catch most flies that came his way and he got in some good home runs, too. Even the kids who had thrown rocks at him and his sisters and called them names, were happy to have him on their team.

But there was one thing he needed if he was going to improve his game and maybe have a shot at becoming a baseball star like that baseball player he'd read about in the newspaper, Willie Mays, Rookie of the Year. And that was a good baseball glove.

One Saturday afternoon, after he'd finished delivering his newspapers, he jogged down the hill to Pearson's Hardware store on Lonsdale Avenue. He patted his jeans pocket where he had a wad of dollars he'd earned from his paper route.

He walked down the aisle to the sports section and, right away, he saw what he wanted. A genuine, all-leather, hand-stitched Rawlings Special Edition baseball glove. He whistled when he saw the price tag. That glove would use up practically all his savings.

"Can I help you, son?" an elderly clerk said.

"I want a glove," Harry said. "That one." He pointed to the Rawlings.

"Well now, son. That's our most expensive model. It's a Special Edition. Not many of those around. We've got some others here. Not so pricey."

"No. That's the one I want."

"Well, let's see if we've got your size here. Yep. This is it. Last one in stock." The clerk unpacked the glove from its box and gently stroked its shiny black leather. "Want to try it on?"

The glove fit Harry's hand snugly. The leather smelled earthy but it was quite stiff when he tried to open and close his hand.

"What you want to do is work the leather, son," the clerk told him. "The more you work it, the softer it'll get and the better it'll fit your hand."

"Work it?"

"They sell this special Rawlings Gold Glove Butter here but, between you and me, any oil will do just as well. Rub some plain Vaseline into the leather, and the more you use the glove, the better it'll get. Tell you what. I'll throw in a baseball for you. Free."

"Gosh, thanks ... um ... sir." Harry grinned at the elderly man. He sure was nice. Although the beautiful glove was going to use up most of his paper route money, Harry knew it was going to be worth it.

After buying it and taking it home, he spent hours in his room, oiling his new glove with Vaseline, rubbing it into all the creases and crevices until the leather softened. He pounded it with his fist, making a good deep pocket in it. He even tied his glove around his new baseball with string and slept with it under his mattress at night. Soon, when he was playing baseball at school and he went to catch a ball, it was as if the glove captured it. And it stayed right there, in the pocket, until he pulled it out.

Thinking more about Willie Mays, the New York Giants Rookie of the Year, Harry practiced pitching the ball until his pitching was as fast and accurate as a torpedo. And with his new glove, he could catch anything that came his way. Although his batting wasn't always great, when he did hit the ball, he was like a streak of lightning running around the bases. Soon, not only did the other kids want him on on their team, he became the first one they chose.

One of his classmates, Ray Wickland, also had a paper route, so Harry and Ray often walked from school to the paper shack together. Ray was a tall boy with long legs and big hands. And he loved baseball as much as Harry did.

"Hey, Harry," Ray called out to him one day as he was leaving the school grounds after school. "Wait up."

Harry slowed down while Ray caught up.

"I just heard from Joe that they're looking for ballplayers for a team to join the community league. Want to join up?"

"But we've got our paper routes," Harry said.

"The games are all on Saturday mornings."

"Great! Where do I sign up?"

"Joe said you just have to show up for tryouts at St. Andrew's Park at 9:00 next Saturday."

"That's the park down on 11th, right?"

"Right."

Both Ray and Harry made the team, as well as a few other boys in their class at school. To Harry's relief, no one made any comments about the color of his skin. The only thing the managers seemed to care about was if you could play the game or not.

The team became known as the North Van All-Stars. After Harry pitched several shut-outs, he was named one of their star players. The North Van All-Stars won the play-offs and came home with the pennant. Each team member was given their own smaller pennant.

While Harry tacked his pennant onto the wall above his bed, he thought about Willie Mays and wondered if that was how he got his start, by playing in a community league.

CHAPTER 10

About a year after they moved to their new house in North Vancouver, life was going along all right. Harry was at Sutherland Junior High School now and his sisters were still attending the same elementary school. The girls had a few friends who'd come over sometimes after school. As long as they weren't noisy, they were allowed to play with their paper dolls and board games in their bedroom.

The neighbors still weren't very friendly, though. The mothers never came over for tea as neighbors often had in St. Boniface. But Harry's mom was kept pretty busy with all the housework, plus looking after Barton who, now that he could walk, was turning out to be a difficult toddler who needed constant minding.

After school, Harry continued with his paper route, now grown to fifty customers. That meant he was earning fifty cents a day. He had his own bank account and extra spending money for comics, or even going to the movies occasionally for a Saturday matinee with his friend Ray.

They had changed the system at the newspaper shack. Now when the papers arrived, they were already sorted into the individual routes. As soon as the supervisor cut the binding wire around his pile, Harry quickly counted the papers to be sure there were fifty copies and he hadn't been shorted. Then he loaded twenty-five into each of his two newspaper bags, one for each shoulder, and he took off.

He didn't have a bike like most of the other kids, but he could run like wildfire. He raced around his whole route in hilly North Vancouver, tossing the newspapers up onto porches or tucking them into post boxes. Up and down steep stairs and driveways, he sprinted to each house on his route, trying to break his record of getting the whole thing done in under an hour. By the end, he sure was puffed. But every day he was another fifty cents richer.

And every day, his lungs and legs were that much stronger.

Their father continued working as a porter on the trains so he was still often away from home for a week or so at a time. Whenever he left for one of his shifts, he still always reminded Harry to look after his sisters and the rest of the family.

One winter night when his father was away, Harry woke up. Something was wrong. It took Harry a few minutes to figure it out. It was the smell.

Smoke! He smelled smoke. Something was burning!

He flung off his covers and flew to the kitchen. He flicked on the overhead light. Smoke was billowing from the old electric stove. Had it been left turned on? In the window nearby, his mom's new curtains were on fire.

Harry dashed to his sisters' room, banging on the door. "Wake up, you guys! You have to wake up! The kitchen's on fire!"

"What? What's happening?" Carolyn cried, running into the hallway in her nightgown. Valerie was right behind her.

Harry beat on his mom's door and flung it open. He switched on the overhead light. That woke his little brother who started screaming. He stood in his crib with his arms raised, begging to be picked up. Carolyn lifted him out but he still didn't stop crying, even though she gave him his favorite blanket.

Amazingly, Harry's mom was still asleep. How could she sleep with all that racket? Must be those new sleeping pills the doctor had given her. Harry had to shake her shoulder. "Mom! Mom! There's a fire!"

Finally she rolled over, blinking up at him. "What?"

"There's a fire!" Harry shouted at her. "The kitchen. Fire! It's on fire!"

That caught her attention. She bolted upright, pulling the blanket around her back. "No! That's terrible! Where's the baby?" She rushed to his empty crib. "Where is he?"

"Carolyn's got him. He's all right."

His mom grabbed her slippers and followed Harry out into the hallway.

Smelly, dark smoke curled around the ceiling. The fire was a lot worse now. In an instant, the hallway had become filled with so much smoke they could hardly see the walls. The fire in the kitchen was crackling and popping. Waves of heat rolled over Harry's face. The smoke was suffocating.

"Mom!" Harry shouted, his heart racing. "What do we do?"

His mom just stood there staring through the smoke at the fire, shaking her head, her eyes huge. She looked stunned. She didn't know what to do any more than he did.

Harry's father's voice echoed in Harry's ears. "Look after your mother and sisters." It was up to him to do something in this emergency. But what?

"Don't we have to phone the fire department or something?" Carolyn yelled over Barton's screams. She was trying to bounce him up and down to make him stop crying, but he was really scared. Tears streamed down his nose and red cheeks. He tried to hide his face behind the scrap of blanket he always carried around.

"How?" Harry shouted back. "We haven't got a phone." Smoke was stinging his eyes and throat, making him cough. It was hard to breathe. "But we've all got to get out of here. Now. Right now. It's not safe."

Since they couldn't reach the back door in the kitchen, they had go out the front door which they rarely used.

"Come on, you guys. Hurry! We got to hurry."

Harry urged his mom and sisters to climb over the boxes and piles of paper in the front hall. He tripped over an old leather pair of his father's shoes. He shuffled them on and grabbed a jacket, also his father's. He tried to open the front door.

Of course the lock was sticky. Everyone was pressed behind him, their voices frantic. "Hurry! Unlock the door! Unlock it."

Finally, Harry got it unlocked. He tugged the door open. Then he followed his family out of the house, stumbling down the steps to the front yard, coughing and coughing. He pulled in a deep breath of cold, fresh night air and coughed some more.

He stood in the front yard with his family, rubbing his

stinging eyes and staring back at their house. It was dark out, but he could see smoke streaming out the front door, and the living room windows flickered with light from the fire.

"Maybe we should have tried to put out the fire," Harry's mom said, slumping down on the large rock beside their front gate and pulling the blanket closer around her back.

"We couldn't. It was too big," Harry told her. "Val, you got to go next door. Ask them to call the fire department for us."

"Me? Why me?"

"The guys next door like you. They let you play with Marilyn. Go. Now. You got to go quick." He was yelling now, pulling her arm. "Come on. Hurry. Before it's too late."

He went with her up to the neighbor's gate while the rest of the family waited in their front yard. Valerie crept up the sidewalk and timidly knocked on the door.

"Hurry, Val! Hurry!" Harry yelled, pacing on the front sidewalk.

"They're not answering," she called back to him.

"You got to knock louder!" Harry shouted. "I can see flames coming out the window now."

Finally, someone came to the door. Harry thought it was Marilyn's dad. Harry saw Valerie pointing to the fire at their house and nodding her head.

The man shut the door. Valerie came back up to the street to join him.

"What did he say?" Harry said.

"He said fine. He'll phone the fire department."

For a long time, no one said anything. They all just stood there, staring at the fire as it licked at the outside walls. Smoke billowed out the roof and sparks flew up into the dark sky like falling stars. Harry couldn't believe this was happening. Right here. His own house. Soon, everything they owned would be lost. It was even worse than when their house was flooded in St. Boniface.

Had he done the right thing? Maybe his mom was right. Maybe he should have put out the fire when he first saw it instead of running away from it. He could have at least tried.

Even little Barton was quiet now. Carolyn was still holding him, jiggling him up and down and he was looking around with his big round eyes as if he couldn't believe what he was seeing, either. The noise of the fire was really loud, whooshing, crackling, and banging. Soon the thick smoke and intense heat drove them out into the street.

"So why aren't the firemen here yet?" Carolyn said.

"Maybe the fire department's way on the other side of town,"

Harry said. "It'll take them a while to get here." He couldn't remember seeing a fire station anywhere in their neighborhood. He was starting to worry, too. If they didn't get here soon, there'd be nothing left of their house. He looked down the hill. There was no sign of a fire engine's flashing red light.

There was a loud crash. He swung around to see part of the roof caving in as the fire climbed onto the roof. People from across the street streamed over to watch.

"Did you call the fire department?" a man called out to Harry.

"Yes, they should be here soon."

In the distance, he saw a red light flashing and a siren wailing.

"That must be them now," he said, feeling relieved.

But it wasn't a fire truck. It was a police car. It skidded to a stop in front of the house. Two police officers hurried out.

"Anyone left in the house?" one of them asked Harry's mom.

"No." She shook her head and pulled the blanket closer again. She sighed and shut her eyes as if she couldn't stand the sight of everything around her. Her cheeks were wet with tears.

"Good. Good," the police officer said. "But you're too close to the fire, Ma'am. Look. Why don't you come and wait in the car?" He helped her up from the rock and ushered her into the back seat of the police car.

Meanwhile, the other police officer was on the car phone, shouting the address. "Yes. A big one …"

More neighbors came out in slippers and robes and blankets to watch the blaze. Above the house, the whole sky glowed red. Then Harry heard more wailing sirens. The firefighters must be on their way. Finally.

The first fire engine screeched to a stop behind the police car and firefighters rushed out. There were four of them, wearing long rubber coats and red helmets.

"Anyone left in there?" the one closest to Harry shouted.

"No," Harry said. "We're all here."

"Good." The firefighter signaled to the others to unload the hoses and attach them to a fire hydrant down the street.

Soon they were spraying the house. Great clouds of steam and smoke rose up into the night with sizzles and crackles and crashes. It was like a giant Halloween fireworks display. Exciting, but Harry wished with all his heart that it wasn't his own family's house that was burning down.

By the time the firemen were finished and the fire was finally out, there wasn't much left of their home. The family wasn't allowed to go back into the house to retrieve anything from the smoldering rubble. Too dangerous, the firefighters told them.

But even in the darkness of the night, Harry could see that practically everything they owned was lost. All his new comics would be gone. Burnt up. As well as his baseball glove. The one he'd saved up for from his paper route until he had enough money to buy the very best, the Rawlings Special Edition. All those hours he'd spent oiling that glove, working the leather until it was as soft as ice cream, were wasted. It would be a long time before he'd ever be able to replace it.

His little brother, Barton, was inside the police car with their mother now, but his sisters were standing together near the back of it. Their heads were down and he knew they must be crying.

That's what he sure felt like doing. But he couldn't. Not in front of all these people.

CHAPTER 11

When the fire was finally out, the neighbors who'd come outside to watch it drifted away, back to their homes. They shut their doors firmly against the Jerome family troubles. Maybe they were even glad that the Jerome house had burnt down, Harry thought. Maybe Marilyn's dad took his time calling the fire station and that's why the firefighters took so long to arrive.

Now their neighborhood could become all-white once again. Harry still harbored bad feelings about that other neighborhood where they'd been asked to move.

The firefighters rolled up their hoses, loaded their ladders onto the sides of their trucks, and got ready to leave.

One of the police officers asked Harry, "Do you have any relatives in town you kids could go and stay with? Any friends? Anyone from school? Any neighbors?"

Harry shook his head, looking at the nearby darkened houses.

He couldn't think of a single family who'd welcome his family to stay. In the more than a year since they'd been living in that house, he didn't think anybody had even once invited his mom over for tea. He had certainly never visited any of the houses himself, except to deliver their newspapers and to collect his money at the end of each month.

If only his father were here. He would know what to do. But he wasn't due home for several days yet. Harry didn't even know how to contact him. On the train there wasn't any phone that he knew of.

He remembered again that his father had put him in charge of the family while he was away. What could he do? Where could they go? They'd just lost everything, every single thing they owned. And it was the middle of the night and …

"Hang on, kid." The police officer patted his shoulder. "I'll put in a call and see if we can find some beds for you."

Harry and his sisters leaned against the police officer's car while he made the call. Harry's mother was sitting inside on the backseat with Barton bundled up in a blanket on her lap, fast asleep. Thank goodness for that, thought Harry. At least he wasn't screaming.

"Beds?" Carolyn sniffed and wiped tears off her cheeks. "We need more than beds. It's dark out. What if starts raining?"

Valerie looked worried, too.

Harry was way too tired to explain that he was sure the beds would be inside somewhere. Inside some shelter.

A few minutes later, the police officer came out of the car and told the kids, "We're sending another car for you. It'll take you to the Salvation Army hospice up the hill. They'll put you up for the night."

The basement in the Salvation Army building was dark and smelled like a toilet that had been cleaned with strong disinfectant. But it was warm and dry and out of the wind. And away from the nose-prickling smoke of the fire.

The police officers left and an elderly caretaker led Harry and his family to a corner of a large room where there were a few chairs and a couch.

"Sorry, but all our beds in the shelter are taken for the night," he said to Harry's mom. "You could use the couch and we'll see what we can do for the kids."

Harry's mom sat down heavily on the couch with Barton still fast asleep in her arms. She gently rocked him back and forth with her eyes closed. Harry hoped his brother would stay asleep because, if he woke up and found he wasn't at home, he'd start screaming for sure.

Harry and his sisters helped the elderly man move some of the wooden chairs together to make sort-of beds for them.

"At least we don't have to sleep on the floor." Carolyn sniffed back tears.

"Or outside," Valerie said.

The man brought them each a thick gray woolen army blanket that they spread out on the chairs. Then they climbed onto the chairs and curled up in the blankets. There weren't any pillows, so Harry turned onto his side and put his arm under his head to support it. He thought he'd never get to sleep on such a hard and uncomfortable surface, but the next thing he knew, he was waking up and the sun was shining through the window above the couch where his mom was still fast asleep. It was morning.

A few days later, their father came home from his shift. With the help of people at the Salvation Army, he found the family another house not far from where they used to live. It was even smaller than their old house, with just two bedrooms, so Harry had to share a room with his sisters again.

The family had lost everything in the fire, so the Salvation Army helped furnish their new house with beds and chairs and a kitchen table. They also provided some clothes for the kids. Harry didn't really care that much about the clothes. As long as he had some good jeans and T-shirts, he was fine. But his sisters complained a lot. They were embarrassed to have to wear old faded and crumpled clothes. One of the teachers at their school gave them some hand-me-downs from her daughter who was older. The clothes were in better shape, but the girls still complained that it was embarrassing to have to wear secondhand clothes to school.

Harry started saving from his newspaper route for another baseball mitt, but he knew he'd probably never get one as good as the Rawlings Special Edition that had been lost in the fire. He still played baseball every chance he got, even though he had to borrow a glove from one of the other players.

CHAPTER 12

That fall when the baseball season was over, Harry and Ray Wickland started playing soccer on the soccer team at school. Harry discovered that he liked soccer just as much as baseball. In fact, maybe he liked it even more. He loved racing along the field, dribbling the soccer ball, out-running everyone. Then making that big hard kick that sometimes scored.

Thank goodness for sports. That and his paper route were the only things that kept Harry going.

The next year, Harry was in Grade 8 at Sutherland Junior High, in an all-boys class. As usual, he was the only non-white student in class and he was also small for his age. He was quiet and still spent most of the time at school with his head down, hoping no one would notice him. He didn't get great marks, just good enough for a passing grade.

But he still loved sports. Pretty well any sport. In soccer, he could be counted on to race down the field, dribbling the ball, and with a good swift kick, often score a goal. In baseball, he continued being a star pitcher in the North Vancouver All-Stars. And when he was at bat and got a hit, he was usually fast enough to get to first base before the ball did. He loved playing basketball and volleyball during gym classes at school.

Maybe he'd inherited some of his grandfather's genes. His mother had told him about her father, John Armstrong Howard.

"Army Howard, they called him," she said. "You know, he went to the 1912 Olympics in Sweden? Represented Canada, he did. First black athlete in Canada in the Olympics. And he should have won, too. If it weren't for a really mean coach, they said he would have come first in his sprints."

It wasn't until Harry was in senior high school that he discovered the sport that ended up changing his life.

In the fall of 1957, when Harry was in Grade 11, a new boy from Toronto arrived. His name was Paul Winn. He was probably the only other Afro-Canadian boy in the entire North Vancouver Senior Secondary School. When people mixed up him and Harry, because they were both Afro-Canadian, Paul laughed his big hearty belly laugh, because no two people could have been more different. Paul was as outgoing, funny, and popular, as Harry was quiet, shy, and reserved. But they had one thing in common. They both loved sports.

At first, they weren't friends. Harry usually left school as soon as the dismissal bell rang and classes were over. Although he didn't have his boyhood paper route any longer, leaving school when classes were over was his usual habit because he still wasn't comfortable socializing. But Paul liked to hang out in the school grounds, shooting hoops on the outdoor basketball court and joking around with a bunch of other classmates.

One day their Social Studies teacher made an announcement to his class. "Hey, fellows—and girls, too," he said. "I'm starting a new club. A track-and-field club. Anyone interested in coming out, meet me in the gym after school."

Harry glanced over at Paul, wondering what he'd say. Paul shrugged and, wiggling his eyebrows, he grinned at Harry. So after school, Harry joined him and a bunch of other fellows and a few girls from their class in the gym.

"All right, let's see what you've got." The teacher led them outside to the schoolyard. After a brief warm-up stretch, the kids were soon jogging around the field. Around and around and around. After a few rounds, most of the guys were panting, slowing down, and holding their sides.

But not Harry. One thing he was used to was running. All those years delivering newspapers, running up and down the steep hills of North Vancouver, trying to get the papers delivered in the shortest possible time, he'd developed good strong legs and good lungs.

"Not bad," the coach said to him. "Now, how about jumping?"

It turned out that Harry was fairly good in high jumping and long jumping. But that's where his new friend, Paul Winn, really shone. In Toronto, before moving to B.C., he'd done some long jumping and also the triple jump, sometimes called the hop, skip, and jump, and he held a number of Canadian student records.

"You're like a jackrabbit out there," one of the kids laughed after his triple jump landed him right out of the sand.

"Mister Jack the Rabbit, that's me," Paul joked, wiggling his nose and waving his fingers on top of his head like rabbit ears.

After a few months training a couple of days a week after school, the coach signed them up for their first competition, the North Vancouver school district invitational track-and-field meet. Other track teams from all the North and West Vancouver high schools had been invited.

It was Harry's first meet and he was nervous. Playing on a baseball or soccer team was completely different from track. In baseball and soccer, you were part of a whole team and you could blend in. But in track and field, the entire focus of everyone's attention was totally on each person competing. And in a race or a jump, that person was him. Yikes! The thought of everyone's eyes on him made the skin on the back of his neck prickle.

After the 100-yard sprint had been called, he stood nervously at the starting line, stretching his legs and his back. He glanced down the row of other competitors. They all looked a lot calmer than he felt. He had a glob of spit lodged in his throat. He swallowed hard. It didn't help. He could hardly breathe.

The starter shouted, "On your marks. Get set. Go!"

Harry wasn't ready. He kind of stumbled at the starting line before taking off. He ran his hardest down the track behind the pack of other runners straining toward the finish line. He ended up fourth or fifth. He didn't bother asking.

His coach was there, shaking his head. "Thought you'd at least place in the first three, Jerome."

"Right." Harry knew he should have done better. It was that bad start. He'd have to concentrate on that.

"We'll try you out in the relay," the coach said. "You won't have to worry so much about the start."

Harry nodded.

"You can run the third leg. It's the toughest but you've got the speed. Paul can bring us home."

The team hadn't practiced passing the baton so they weren't that smooth. But they came in third. Not bad for their first relay.

"Maybe we have something here we can build on," the coach said.

Over the next months, the track team continued to meet a couple of times a week after school to work out. Harry concentrated on two things: his start in the sprints and improving passing the baton in the relay.

His start got better and better. And the relay team learned to pass the baton without slowing down or fumbling. It also became much smoother.

One afternoon, the coach told his athletes he wanted them to try a new technique he'd read about. "What I want you to do is visualize the whole race before actually running it."

"Visualize it?" Paul asked.

"Right," the coach went on. "Before running, I want you to think hard about each step along your race. From the start where you explode out of the blocks, all the way down the track, and right to the finish. Imagine yourself sprinting, digging down, and pushing off with your toes. And keep those arms pumping hard and fast to set the pace …"

Harry tried the visualizing thing but, the trouble was, he couldn't concentrate completely on the race. There was always some part of his mind that was self-conscious, always thinking about people staring at him, and wondering what they might be thinking of him.

His actual running was smooth. So smooth, it looked effortless, people said. And usually he wasn't even breathless at the end of a 100- or 200-yard sprint. Delivering newspapers as fast as he could had been excellent training for a sprinter. He knew exactly how to turn on the speed.

In March 1959, when Harry was in Grade 12, the coach organized another meet to be held at the school on a Saturday. Eighteen-year-old Harry was nervous, as usual. It was one of the first real track-and-field meets of the season. As his coach suggested, he'd bought himself a new pair of "spikes," leather running shoes, with money he'd managed to scrape together from doing odd jobs around the neighborhood. The shiny black shoes had short metal spikes in the soles that helped him dig into the cinder track and they were a perfect fit, enclosing his feet snugly.

When they announced the final heat for the 100-yard dash, Harry went to the starting line. He glanced at the other competitors. They were anxiously stretching their legs, shaking their arms, trying to relax. He was anxious as well, but he took in a deep calming breath, and stared down the track. He imagined himself running, putting on the power all the way from the starting line to the finish, concentrating on getting those knees up and legs churning, like a locomotive speeding down the railway tracks. Faster, faster, and faster.

"On your marks!" the starter shouted.

Harry pulled in another breath and joined the other guys, standing at their starting blocks.

"Get set."

This time Harry shut out thoughts about everyone else. The crowd, the other competitors, even his coach.

He lowered one knee to the cinder track, planted his foot firmly against the starting block. He took in a third deep breath, expanding his chest, and stared down at the finish line.

Now there was just him and that thin strand of wool stretched across the track.

"Go!"

He pushed hard and burst out of the blocks, pumping his arms, pounding his feet into the cinders, eyes on the prize.

Push, push, push. Faster, faster, faster. All the way down the track.

Until he hit the finish line and cut through the strand of wool like a knife slashing through butter.

First! He was sure that this time he'd come first.

In fact, he was way out in front.

The crowd exploded. They cheered, yelling, "Harry, Harry, Harry …"

It turned out that not only had Harry come first in the race, he'd also equaled the speed of renowned sprinter Percy Williams's provincial Inter High School record for the 100-yard dash, with a time of 10 seconds flat. That was a record that had stood since 1927. For 32 years!

That day, Harry had his first taste of victory.

And it was sweet as honey.

Later that day, Harry and three of his teammates lined up for the 4 x 100 yard relay. The toughest portion was the third.

"You run that for us, Harry," their coach said. "And you can bring us home, Paul."

Harry and his three teammates had been practicing the "hand-offs," where they had to pass the baton from one teammate to the other. Today, their hand-offs were perfect, smooth, without a hitch. Harry ran his leg of the race all out, so they were way ahead when he passed the baton to Paul. Paul gave it all he had. And their team went on to win the gold medal.

Again, the stands exploded with cheers as all the guys on the team walloped each other's backs and danced around, whooping.

"We did it," Paul chanted. "We are the champions!"

Someone in the stands that afternoon had a particular interest in the relay team. That young man's name was John Minichiello. Yes, he was thinking. Those are the kind of athletes we want for our Optimist Striders. He and his friend, Milton Wong, had recently formed a track-and-field club for youth with funding help from the local Optimists Service Club. John was the coach and Milton was the manager.

After the awarding of the gold medals, John approached the relay team and invited them to join his new track-and-field club. Paul Winn was enthusiastic. And his enthusiasm, as usual, was contagious.

"Okay," Harry said. "Could my sister join, too?"

"Your sister?" John Minichiello peered at Harry over his glasses.

"Her name's Valerie. She's just fourteen, but she can jump higher and run faster than any other kid at her school."

"Sure. Bring her along next Monday. We'll give her a try. See what she can do."

So began Harry Jerome's career as one of the most famous and successful track-and-field athletes in B.C., ever. And in all of Canada, as well.

But things would not always go as smoothly as they had that day.

CHAPTER 13

When Harry got home that afternoon, his sisters were in the bedroom. Carolyn was sitting on her bed and Valerie was behind her, braiding her hair.

"Ouch," Carolyn squealed, pulling away. "That hurt."

"Look," Valerie huffed. "Either you want me to braid your hair or not."

"All right. But try not to pull it so hard."

"Sorry to interrupt your hairdressing, ladies," Harry said. "But how would you like to join a real track-and-field club, Val?"

"A real track-and-field club? What are you talking about?"

"A coach named John Minichiello invited Paul Winn and me and some other guys to join his new track club. And I asked him if you could join, too."

"Really? What did he say?"

"He said, 'Sure.' Come and try out after school on Monday."

"But what if I'm not good enough?"

"I know you're good enough, Val. Didn't you beat all the kids at your school at the last track meet? Even the boys?"

Valerie shrugged. "Maybe."

"Don't be such a scaredy-cat. You won't know if you don't try, right? Right?"

"All right. I'll go to the tryouts on Monday. Maybe."

"Now can Valerie finish my hair?" Carolyn said. "I have to leave soon. I'm meeting some friends for a movie."

"All right, all right," Harry said. "What's for supper?"

The following Monday after school, Paul Winn, Harry, and Valerie piled into the car owned by fellow athlete George Mason. They drove from North Vancouver, across the Lion's Gate Bridge to Stanley Park and Brockton Oval where there was a cinder track. That's where they would be training with the Optimist Striders and their new coach, John Minichiello.

The first day they arrived with their shorts and T-shirts in their knapsacks, John was waiting for them on the track with a team of other teens he'd been training. John welcomed the new members to the club and told them about their schedule. He was a short, powerfully built man with sandy hair, thick glasses, and a deep voice that carried right across the field.

While Harry listened to the coach, he eyed the eight-lane cinder track that had been laid in an oval around a big grassy field. He was itching to start running around that track. Tall shrubs and a hedge enclosed the track on three sides and there was a set of wooden bleachers on the other. Under the bleachers were dimly-lit washrooms and showers.

"We'll be meeting here three times a week after school, from four until six," John said. "Most of the meets I'll be signing you up for will be on the weekends so they won't interfere with school. Now, let's warm up. That way I'll see what you've got."

After they ran around the track a few times, he led them through a series of stretching and warm-up exercises. Harry had never done such serious and extensive stretching before. When he used to deliver newspapers, he usually just loaded up his papers and took off, running his fastest around the whole route.

Finally, John let them loose.

"I want you guys to run around the track a couple more times to really get warmed up."

Harry took off, leading the pack around the track. That felt good.

Next John introduced them to high-knees drills where they

ran lifting their knees as high as they could with each step. Harry could feel the muscles at the back of his thighs stretching painfully with the effort, but he kept on going, faster, faster. When he saw that his sister was trying to keep up, he put even more effort into getting down to the finish.

John was there, nodding. "You two are going to be fine. Just fine." His glasses glinted as he pointed to them.

Harry could see that Valerie was relieved. She gave him a small smile.

"Now," their coach said, "for something completely different."

He opened up a sack and pulled out a bunch of green cotton vests. Handing them around to the kids, he said, "I want you to put these on. We're going to try some exercises while you're wearing them."

Harry found his vest surprisingly heavy. When he tied it on, it pulled his shoulders down. When he looked more closely, he saw that the four front pockets of the vests were loaded with weights.

John led them through other exercises, running backwards, hopping on one foot, then intervals where they ran around the track, jogging for fifty steps, then running all out for fifty steps, then back to jogging. Then the most strenuous exercise of all, running sideways, taking big steps like their legs were giant scissors opening and closing.

"Come on, guys," John urged, clapping his hands together. "Faster, faster, faster …"

The weights in the pockets bounced against Harry's chest, but he kept going, going, going. Sweat poured down his forehead and into his eyes, stinging them. Now he understood why some of the older guys wore headbands. His legs ached but he didn't let up for a second. He noticed Valerie was really pushing herself as well.

During the whole routine, coach John was watching them, glancing down at his stopwatch, making notes on his clipboard. After what seemed like an hour but may have been only a few minutes, he blew his whistle and called the athletes to gather round.

"Good start, you guys. Excellent. Don't forget to tuck your elbows in, Harry. You're flopping them around like chicken wings."

Harry nodded, and made a note to himself about his elbows.

"Now, what I want you to do," the coach said, "is take off your vests."

Harry pulled off his vest and tossed it into the big canvas bag along with the others. He jumped a couple of times and was amazed at how light and free he felt.

"Wow!" Paul said. "Bet I could fly if I tried hard enough."

Harry nodded. That's how he felt, too.

"Right." The coach clapped his hands together. "Now we're going to go through the same routine again."

When Harry ran down the track, he felt so light that it would have taken just a tiny bit more effort to wing it over the whole stadium.

This time when they went through their routine, everyone was grinning. It was so effortless and easy. Even the grueling scissor side running.

Eventually, the coach blew his whistle. "Six o'clock," he called out. "Time to pack it in."

Harry joined the others, gathering his belongings, pulling on his track top and bottoms.

"Fun, eh?" Paul grinned at him and slapped his back.

Harry nodded.

"Looks like your sister had a good time, too."

Valerie was talking and laughing with a couple of other girls at the high-jumping pit. They were dragging the landing mats across the track into the storage area under the wooden bleachers.

Now, how were they going to get back home to North Vancouver, Harry was wondering. George had had to leave early.

"Anyone need a ride to the north shore?" the coach called out.

Harry put up his hand. The coach nodded.

"Can my sister come, too?"

"Yes siree, bub." The coach grinned at him. "So how was that workout for you?"

"Good," Harry said, waving his sister to join them.

"Hey, Mr. Minichiello, I got to ask you something," Paul said, as they were walking out to the parking lot.

"What's that?"

"Where did you get the idea of doing a workout with those weighted vests? We never had anything like that back in the track club in Toronto. Or in the high school track club in North Van, either."

The coach smiled at him. "The idea came from a friend of mine, Doug Hepburn. You heard of him?"

"Sure," Harry said. "He's a world champion weightlifter who lives in Vancouver, right?"

"But he isn't in track, though, is he?" Paul said.

"No, but do you know that he can jump over nine feet from a standing start? Pretty impressive for a guy who weighs over 250 pounds. So I got to thinking that he must have very strong legs. And the way he got so strong was … what?" He looked at the athletes gathered around him.

One kid Harry didn't know yet, whose name turned out to be Gary, said, "Lifting weights?"

"Right. So I got to thinking that if you have real strong legs, then you'll be able to not only jump farther and higher, but you should also be able to run all that much faster, too. What do you guys think?"

Harry found himself nodding along with the other kids. Made sense to him. And he loved that feeling of flying down the track after he'd taken off the weights. It was the same feeling he used to get on his jog home, after he'd delivered all his newspapers and his bags were empty and he was suddenly about ten pounds lighter. Exactly the same feeling. As if in one giant leap, he'd be able to reach the clouds.

The two-hour training session had been exhausting, but now it seemed to Harry that the time had flown by so quickly, he was already looking forward to the next session.

"What do you think about the club?" Paul Winn asked them, after the coach had dropped Harry, Valerie, and him off at the bottom of the hill in North Vancouver. They were walking the rest of the way home.

"It's good," Harry said. "Real good. Sure am starving, though. Wonder what Mom's cooking for supper tonight."

"You've got a one-track mind, Harry," Valerie laughed. "Always thinking about food. Think the coach will let me join up?"

"Don't see why not." Paul smiled at her. "Today I saw how high you can jump, Val. You can jump higher than all the other girls and they're all older than you. Better watch out or they're going to start calling *you* Mr. Jack the Rabbit, instead of me."

When Valerie grinned back at Paul, her whole face lit up Like there was a bright light shining through her eyes.

Harry thought he'd never seen his sister look happier in her whole life.

That's exactly how he felt, too. The world of track was one place where they fit in. One place where they both really and truly belonged. And where, for the first time, he felt part of a community where your color made no difference to your being accepted.

CHAPTER 14

That spring, the young athletes trained hard at Brockton Oval. John Minichiello was so pleased with their progress, he signed them up for all the local track-and-field meets.

Harry ran the sprints, the 100 yards, and the 200 yards, winning race after race with what looked like an effortless stride. His running technique was as smooth as milk, a bystander observed.

And young Valerie was beating girls two or three years older than herself in competition, both in the 60-yard and 100-yard sprints, as well as in high jumping.

Their friend, Paul Winn, was also seeing success, in long jumping and his favorite event, the triple jump.

It was soon clear that both Jeromes were exceptionally talented athletes. Not only were they talented, but they also had drive. They wanted, more than anything, to win. They were hardworking and always determined to do their very best. Belonging to the Optimist

Striders track club was special for them both. Competing in track and field was a place where, one day, they might achieve their dream of being admired rather than shunned.

But before that, it was going to take a lot of hard work.

Their father was still working long shifts as a porter so he was still away a lot. But when he came home and heard how well Harry and Valerie were doing in track, he nodded and grinned. "One of these days, I'm going to have to be at one of those meets to see you winners with my own eyes." When he leaned over to hug them both, Harry realized for the first time that he was actually taller than their father now. And Valerie was at least as tall as him.

On May 27, 1959, there was a big track meet at Empire Stadium in Vancouver. Harry broke another of Percy Williams's records. He ran the 200 meters in 21.9 seconds, breaking Williams's world record of 22 seconds, set in the 1928 Olympics. It was a record that had stood for 31 years.

That's when people started noticing Harry. They noticed this young kid was consistently coming in first in the 100 yards/meters and 200 yards/meters sprints. And the relay team, with Paul Winn, Harry, and his other teammates from North Van High, was winning gold all over the region, including at meets held as far away as Washington State.

John Minichiello raised the stakes, taking his young athletes to more provincial championships. They came away with medals there, too. It looked as though John's innovative training methods, including those using weights, were working.

So he raised the stakes even higher. He entered some of his most promising athletes into national competitions where they would be competing against athletes from right across Canada.

This was an exciting time for Harry and his teammates. Some of them had never traveled much beyond Vancouver and the lower mainland. Now they were traveling to track meets right across the country. And Harry continued to win almost all his races. For example, in July 1959, in Winnipeg, Manitoba, at the Canadian championships, Harry won the 100-meter race with a time of 10.4 seconds. That was a world-class time.

That's when whispers of "Canada's fastest man" began.

His friend Paul said, "Hey, man. What's all this I've been hearing about Canada's fastest man? That's what I read in the paper."

Harry shrugged. "Just going out there and trying my best," he said, grinning back. But Harry found it really hard to believe that all the attention was directed at him. It was like a dream to find something he loved doing so much. And the bonus was that he might be pretty good at it. But maybe the best part was that now when he walked around, he could hold his head up high. Instead of shunning him, people were starting to look at Harry with increased respect. He wondered if Valerie had also noticed a difference in the way people were treating her, but he never got around to asking her.

Late that summer, Coach Minichiello took Harry to Eugene, Oregon, to compete against some of America's top sprinters in a regional track-and-field meet. There, Harry won the 100-yard dash in 9.5 seconds, setting a new state record.

The following year, in 1960, the Canadian Olympic Trials were being held in Saskatoon, Saskatchewan, in early July. John thought some of his young athletes might be ready to compete at a world-class level. Harry and Valerie were selected. Harry was nineteen at the time and his sister was barely sixteen, one of the youngest competitors.

After traveling from Vancouver to Saskatoon by train a few days before, they were both eager to do their best.

"I'm so excited. This is the big one," Valerie said to Harry as they tucked into a hearty lunch in a restaurant across the street from the track. She could hardly sit still.

"Yes," he said, slicing into a thick, juicy steak. "Rome Olympics, here we come!" He took in a deep breath to calm his churning stomach. He'd already run the qualifying heats for the 100-meter and 200-meter sprints, and his times had been good enough to win him a spot in the final heats that afternoon.

"Right!" Valerie clinked her Coke glass against his and grinned. "Good luck." She crossed fingers on both hands for good luck.

He grinned back. "And good luck to you, kiddo."

In spite of the heavy and quite inappropriate diet that later athletes would have frowned upon as pre-race food, both Valerie and Harry did well that sunny afternoon, and made the Canadian team for the Olympic Games. In fact, Harry ran the 100-meter sprint in his best time ever. Ten seconds flat. Officials were astounded. That time equaled the *world* record set a few months earlier by Armin Hary from Germany.

On that day, July 16, 1960, nineteen-year-old Harry was declared to be one of the fastest men, not just in Canada, but on earth!

Valerie also did well. She qualified for the 100-meter sprint as well as the 4 x 100-meter relay team.

Now all Harry and Valerie had to do was stay healthy and continue training for the rest of the summer for the Olympic Games in Rome at the end of August.

Who would ever have thought these ordinary kids who'd grown up in North Vancouver were going to the Olympic

Games to compete for Canada against the best athletes in the entire world?

Harry shook his head. He still had trouble believing this was all happening to him.

One Friday afternoon, Harry was at the kitchen table eating a peanut butter sandwich when the phone rang.

His sister Carolyn beat him to answering it.

"Mr. Harry Jerome? Sorry, he's away at work and won't be back until next week. Who's calling, please?" she asked as she'd been instructed.

"Oh, *that* Harry Jerome." She made a face and handed the receiver to Harry.

"Who is it?" he whispered.

"Don't know," she shrugged.

"Hello?" His mouth was full of peanut butter.

"Harry Jerome?"

"Yes."

It was a popular local radio station calling.

"We'd like to congratulate you on winning at the tryouts in Saskatchewan and making the Olympic team to represent Canada," the radio guy said.

"Um … thanks."

"So we want to come and do an interview with you tomorrow for our sports special on Sunday about one of the fastest people on earth. Would two o'clock work for you?"

"Ah … ah … sure. I guess." Harry couldn't think of any excuse, except that he'd planned to play basketball with some of his friends on the outdoor courts at school the next day.

"Great. We'll see you tomorrow afternoon."

When his friends heard he was going to be interviewed on the radio, they decided to come over to watch.

"It's going to be such a riot," Paul Winn said.

The next day at lunch, Harry was so nervous he could barely eat. He went into the bathroom and saw his dad's Brylcreem hair lotion on the shelf above the sink. The radio jingle ran through his head: *"Brylcreem. You look so debonair."*

He squeezed some cream onto his palm and worked it into his hair. Then he combed it down until his usually frizzy hair was lying flat and shiny against his scalp. He stared at himself in the mirror and grinned. "Lookin' good," he told himself.

The doorbell rang. It was two men wearing suits. One of the men had a suitcase that turned out to contain a tape recorder, and the other was carrying a couple of microphones.

"Hey, Harry," the suitcase guy said. "We're here for the radio interview. Can we come in?"

"Sure, come on in." Harry tried to look calm and cool in spite of his fluttering stomach. He led them into the living room where Carolyn was practicing on the piano.

"This is my sister," Harry told the men.

Carolyn pointed at Harry's flattened hair and tittered, "Hee, hee, hee."

He glared at her while one of the newspaper men asked, "Is she the jumper who's also going to the Olympics? She got a bronze medal in the Pan-American games last summer. Maybe we could interview her, too?"

"No, this is Carolyn. Hey, Val," Harry called. "These guys from the radio want to meet you."

Valerie came into the living room with a shy smile and the radio men introduced themselves.

She nodded nervously at them and sat on the piano bench beside Harry.

"So, I'll just plug in my tape recorder and we can get the interview started—if that's fine with you, Harry."

"Sure, sure." Harry was suddenly aware how lame his voice sounded. He sounded more like a teenage girl than the almost twenty-year-old guy he was. He cleared his throat and tried to speak in a lower tone. "You can plug it in behind that lamp over there."

The doorbell rang again. It was Paul this time, with a couple of friends, Frankie and Gary, with their basketballs and their new high-top basketball shoes.

"Nice hair," Paul said, grinning.

"Shut up," Harry said.

"Thought we'd come by and watch the interview," Paul said.

"Sure, sure. Come on in."

On his way back to the living room, Harry heard his mom talking to the radio guys.

"Oh, yes. We've always been real proud of our Harry," she was telling them. "And of the girls as well, of course," she added.

"Harry and Valerie have certainly been doing well on the track. Do they take after you? Were you a runner in high school, too?"

"No, no. My husband and me, we're not in the least athletic. I mean, my husband's probably in better shape than I am, running around the trains where he works, you know. Harry takes after my father, though. And Valerie, too. Same build. They both got those long legs. And the drive to win. Yes. They're both pretty good athletes."

"Your father?"

"Yes, yes. You probably heard about him. John Armstrong Howard?"

One of the radio men nodded.

"Army Howard, they called him," Harry's mom went on. "He competed for Canada as a sprinter in the 1912 Olympics in Sweden. And he should have won, but that coach, well, he really had it in for him. Called him all kinds of nasty names, picked on him, you know … wouldn't even allow him to eat with the rest of the athletes."

She went on talking about her father and how he'd grown up in Winnipeg and was the first Canadian of African heritage ever to be in the Olympics, and saying again how he should have won.

For once, Harry was glad his mom could sometimes be such a chatterbox. All he had to do was just sit there and not say a thing.

His friend Paul was perched on the couch armrest and bouncing his basketball back and forth on his knees. His other friends soon became restless, standing around the living room. The radio guys frowned at them when they bounced their basketballs against the wall, so they went outside. Harry followed them, and they started dribbling the balls along the front sidewalk.

"So, you coming up to the school to shoot some hoops?" Paul asked him.

"Sure, I'll just tell those guys in there."

When Harry went back inside, one of the reporters waved a list at him. "We've got a few questions here for you, Harry."

"Okay." Harry sat back down on the piano bench beside Valerie. He was sweating from nerves and the Brylcreem was starting to trickle down his forehead into his eyes.

"When did you start running, Harry?"

Harry shrugged, wiping his stinging eyes with his shirttail. "Guess I've been running all my life."

His mom chimed in. "Harry's always been an active kid. Loved sports since he was knee-high to a grasshopper. Maybe baseball's his favorite. He was in the North Van All-Stars, you know. They even won a pennant."

"What do you think your chances are at the Olympics in Rome?"

"Um ... well ... um ... I'm sure going to try my hardest," Harry said.

After a few other questions about his training and his coaches, the reporter said, "Do you have any advice to give other athletes?"

"Um ... advice." Harry remembered his Cub Scout motto. "'Always do your best,'" he quoted. He could see his friends just outside the living room window. Paul was motioning him to come on out. He nodded at him, trying to wave him away.

"And how about you, Val?" the reporter asked Valerie. "Any advice you can give young athletes?"

"Ah … I like Harry's advice. Always try your best."

"Well, that about wraps it up." The reporter clicked off the microphone. "Thanks for the interview, Harry. You, too, Val. And good luck at the Olympics in Rome." He got up and shook Harry's hand. And Valerie's, too.

Harry hoped he wouldn't notice how sweaty his hand was.

At least now he could finally leave to shoot some hoops with his friends.

CHAPTER 15

One skill Harry was taught early in his running career was the importance of focusing on the task at hand. That is, focusing on running the best race he possibly could. Unfortunately, this total focus caused major problems for Harry with newspaper and radio sports reporters.

It started at the Olympic Games in Rome.

Everyone in the world of track and field was convinced that this time, for sure, Canada would be taking home an Olympic medal. Maybe even the Gold in the 100-meter sprint, because Harry had recently run the race in the fastest time in the world. Was he going to do that again in Rome? If he did win, it would be the first Olympic medal in track and field for Canada since 1932, when Duncan McNaughton won Gold in the high jump.

At the end of August in 1960, the weather in Rome was steaming hot. On August 31, it was 40C in the shade. The

Athletes Village where Harry was staying was set quite far from the Olympic Stadium where the preliminaries for the sprints were taking place.

On his way from the village to the stadium that afternoon, Harry's taxi got caught in a huge traffic jam. He was worried he'd be late for his race so he jumped out of the taxi and ran the rest of the way through the city to the stadium.

He arrived hot and dripping with sweat just as they were announcing his heat in the semi-finals for the 100-meter sprint. He didn't have time to do a proper stretch or power down as he liked to do before a race.

He felt that all eyes in the stadium were on him. He knew expectations were high that he'd run well enough to win that gold medal. He tried to look strong and confident. But he also knew that his entire focus should be totally on his race. That meant that he didn't want to talk to anyone at all. And he was definitely not happy about giving pre-game interviews to reporters.

He was already soaked with sweat and his mouth was so dry, his tongue stuck to the back of his teeth. But because his race had been called, he didn't even have time to ask for a drink of water.

As he laced up his spikes and shook out his legs, trying to get them to relax, newspaper reporters from all over the world gathered around him like wasps around a honey pot, buzzing, peppering him with questions. The reporters had noticed that Harry's times were way ahead in all the preliminary heats so far. They wanted to interview him about how he was feeling. They shouted out to him.

"Are you going to give us a win today, Harry?"

"Are you excited?"

"How do you like Rome?"

"Italian food?"

"Have you met the Pope yet?"

Harry turned away from the reporters and tried to ignore them. He was determined to do just one thing: focus on that semi-final race. He *had* to win it. He wanted to visualize the whole race in his head, as his coaches had taught him. From a good fast start, power down the track, right to the end where he'd break through that ribbon at the finish line, winning the race.

That was his only concern.

The reporters couldn't get a good interview with their star athlete, so they were frustrated. They complained, reporting in their articles that Harry was arrogant, conceited, and a big-headed spoiled brat.

Harry tried to close out their irritating voices. Now it was time for the race. His chance to win that Olympic Gold for Canada, for his family, for himself. And prove to all the world that he was really someone who could hold his head high and be proud of who he was.

This was going to be it. He was going to give it his all.

"On your mark …" Harry pulled in a breath and knelt in his starting blocks.

"Get set …" Up came one knee. Suck in another breath.

"Go!"

He exploded out of the blocks. A great start. Leading the pack …

Running down the track. Straining with all his strength toward the finish line. Push, push, push.

This was it. He was the fastest man in the world. He was going to beat even his own record and win this race …

But in a split second his dream collapsed.

He pulled a leg muscle. He stumbled. All the other runners whizzed past him in a blur as he limped to the finish, his face contorted in pain.

He ended up last.

Harry's dream was crushed.

Canada's dream of winning an Olympic gold medal in the

100-meter sprint was dashed. Frustrated sports writers in major newspapers all across Canada called Harry a quitter.

But he knew he wasn't a quitter.

"I just don't know what went wrong," he said to the few reporters who hung around after the race, shaking his head. "My leg. It just flopped. Lost power."

He shut his eyes and covered his face with his hands.

It was the most disappointing day of his life.

CHAPTER 16

But the Cub Scout motto was stuck in his head. "Always do your best."

The one thing Harry knew he could do was run. And run fast. He was determined to get his leg better. And he was going to go out there again and run! And win!

And that's what he did. After some intense physiotherapy, he went back to training hard. John Minichiello gave him a strict schedule to follow daily, paying special attention to the leg that suffered the pulled muscle.

Harry's new coach at the University of Oregon, Bill Bowerman, also had a rigorous training schedule for him. Harry had been offered an athletic scholarship to attend the university there. He was happy to accept the scholarship, fulfilling his childhood dream of attending a university. After less than a year of steady hard work in the exercise room and on the track at the university, Harry surprised everyone.

On May 20, 1961, at a University track meet in Corvallis, Oregon, he ran the 100-yards in an amazing 9.3 seconds, equaling the world record set by Mel Patton in 1948.

That day, Harry became the first man *in the world* to hold world records for *both* the 100-yard and the 100-meter sprints. Ever!

Sportswriters around the world declared him to be "the fastest man on earth."

Harry continued with his studies at the University of Oregon. And he also continued his vigorous training for track. He didn't compete in many races, but those he did, he won easily.

On August 25, 1962, at his home stadium—the Empire Stadium in Vancouver—Harry ran the 100 yards in 9.2 seconds, equaling a new world record set by both Bob Hayes and Frank Budd a few months earlier.

Harry wanted to make up for his disappointing defeat two years before at the Olympics in Rome. So his sights were on the next big prize. That was to win a gold medal for Canada at the British Empire and Commonwealth Games. They were being held in Perth, Australia, later that year, November 22 to December 1, the beginning of the Australian summer.

Saturday, November 24, 1962, was an unbelievably hot day in Perth. To Harry, it felt even hotter than Rome had been on that fateful day when he'd pulled a muscle in the 100-meter sprint and had limped in last.

And the flies in Perth were terrible. Every time he tried to take in a breath, he had to keep his mouth firmly closed or he would have breathed in a cloud of flies. The little pests kept going for his eyes and his sweaty forehead. In spite of the heat and the flies, and a roaring sore throat and cough, Harry had done well so far. He'd won all his preliminary heats, coming in way ahead of any competitors.

So, again, when the final for the 100-yard sprint was called, all eyes were focused on him. As always, wherever he went, sports reporters hounded him.

"How are you feeling, Harry?"

"Is this race in the bag?"

"How's that leg?"

They lined up to pepper him with questions. But he shook his head.

"Not now," he said and tried to wave them away.

He didn't have time for interviews. At that moment, he had to focus on his race. Focus, focus. Give that race everything he had.

But Harry wasn't feeling well that day. He was running a fever and his throat was killing him. He could barely swallow. If one of his coaches had been there, he would probably have told him to go to bed with some antibiotics. But because of lack of funding, neither of his coaches, John Minichiello and Bill Bowerman, had been permitted to attend the Games.

It was time for the big race. Again, the fastest runners in the world were lined up.

"On your mark!" the starter shouted. "Get set ... Go!

They were off.

Harry exploded out of the blocks ahead of the field. Off to a great start.

He powered down the track. Straining hard for the finish. Giving it every ounce of strength he had. Looking fantastic. This was it.

He was going to win Gold for Canada and make up for the Olympics.

He was pushing hard. Harder than he ever had in his life. Every molecule in his body strained toward that finish line.

At the 60-yard mark, he felt a twinge in his thigh.

Suddenly, as if it had been shot with a gun, his left leg collapsed and totally lost power.

Harry managed to drag himself to the finish, coming in last.

Although he didn't know it at the time, he'd suffered a much worse injury than he had in Rome. That day in Perth, he had ruptured a major muscle in his left thigh.

Sports reporters turned away from him in disgust.

Allan Fotheringham reported on the front page of the *Vancouver Sun* in big black headlines: JEROME FOLDS AGAIN. He wrote a blistering account of the race, accusing Harry of quitting just because he was behind the other runners.

Harry was devastated by the negative comments.

But maybe they were right, a small voice inside his head whispered. Maybe, when the chips were down, when the really important race was run and had to be won, maybe he really *was* nothing but a no-good, spoiled-brat quitter.

When the doctors examined his leg, they found that the main muscle in his thigh had ripped and totally pulled away from his knee, leaving a large hollow in his leg. Big enough to put your whole fist in. A ruptured *rectus femoris* muscle was a serious injury that needed immediate surgery to repair it.

One of the doctors at the Games shook his head. "I don't think Harry will ever walk again," he commented.

They hustled Harry onto a plane back home as he requested. When he got back to Vancouver, Doctor Hector Gillespie, a gifted orthopedic surgeon, examined Harry's leg. He decided to operate immediately to try to save it. It was a long and involved operation where he had to reattach the thigh muscles to the knee tendons and ligaments. He worked far into the night. In the end, he refused to submit a bill for this delicate operation, saying that he felt it was a privilege to have worked on such a fine athlete, one of the top runners in the world.

Harry's leg was encased in plaster from hip to toe for over six months to give it time to heal. When the cast was finally removed, his once muscular leg had atrophied to the size of his arm.

Everyone thought he would never walk again.

At first he couldn't. He couldn't put any weight on that leg. There was no strength in it at all.

But Harry persisted, encouraged by Dr. Gillespie, who became a good friend. Harry was determined to recover. He spent months of exhausting work, of physiotherapy and intense care from Coach Minichiello. Eventually, he was not only walking without crutches or a cane, he began to slowly jog around the track, and he gradually put on speed. So much so, that by early 1964—a year and a half after his injury—his coach entered him into a few local races and he did surprisingly well. Especially for someone the doctors had said would never walk again.

By August 1964, Harry's leg was feeling pretty good, so he

traveled to the Olympic trials in Quebec at the Canadian Track and Field Championships, where he ran a spectacular 100-meter race. People were astounded by his recovery. Harry Jerome was well and truly back.

And he certainly qualified to be on the team representing Canada at the Olympics in Tokyo later that year in October. When he ran the 100 meters in the preliminary heats in Tokyo, he surprised everyone by doing well enough to make it to the final.

In the final race, Harry concentrated hard on doing his best. He came in third and won the Bronze. This was a time for celebration because it was Canada's first medal in track and field at the Olympic Games since Duncan McNaughton's Gold in the high jump in 1932.

The press changed its tune. In big headlines they called Harry "Canada's Comeback Kid." For anyone to persevere and to come back after such a major injury as he had experienced in Perth was an astounding achievement. Harry Jerome is an inspiration to all young athletes, they declared. He never gave up. He always did his best.

Harry could have retired honorably from track at this point. He was twenty-four years old. He had competed in the Olympics and had won an Olympic medal for his country.

But he wasn't done yet. He was hungry for that elusive gold medal. So he set his sights on the British Empire and Commonwealth Games in Jamaica in 1966. That would give him almost two years to train.

And train he did. He was relentless in his daily workouts.

Late one rainy autumn night, his friend Paul Winn was about to go to bed when his doorbell rang. It was Harry.

"So, have you done your workout yet today?" Harry asked him.

"Aw … no. I've been busy at work all day and I'm …"

"Come on. Grab your shoes. Let's go." Harry was already jogging on the spot, stretching his arms above his head.

"But it's raining," Paul groaned. "It's dark. It's late."

"So?"

Paul sighed. He tied on his runners, grabbed a jacket, and followed his friend out into the dark, wet night to run around the park.

"Hey, is there no stopping you, Harry?"

"Nothing's going to stop me until I've got my hands on Gold," Harry laughed. "Just one little old gold medal. That's all I want. Then I'll be happy as a lark."

CHAPTER 17

August 8, 1966, was a sizzling hot day in Kingston, Jamaica. Hot even for Jamaica. It was the kind of dense humid heat that made your brain mushy.

Athletes had come from all over the world to compete in the British Empire and Commonwealth Games.

Again, Harry had done well in the preliminary heats of the 100-yard sprints, and now he was at the starting line for the final. Also at the starting line were Tom Robinson from the Bahamas, and the local favorite, Trinidadian sprinter Edwin Roberts. Both had excellent times in their heats.

Harry nodded to them. Then he stretched and nervously shook his legs. Especially that left one that had given him so much grief a few years before in that fateful race in Australia, where everyone expected him to win but where he ended up coming in dead last.

His kid sister Valerie was there in the crowd, right in the front row. He could see her out of the corner of his eye. She was clasping her hands together as if in prayer.

Sweat dripped down Harry's forehead and into his eyes. He brushed them with the back of his hand and told himself to concentrate. Concentrate. That's what he had to do. Visualize the whole race. Right from "On your mark, get set, go." Every step down the track.

He had to raise his hips a little. About two inches should do it, his Oregon coach, Bill Bowerman, had told him. And watch that left elbow. Don't let it clip out. Keep it in close. Keep it all in close. And float down the track. Keep your eyes on the finish line. That's where you're heading. That finish line.

You can do it, he heard his first coach John Minichiello whisper in his ear. You can do it. Do your best. *Your best*, echoed around his head. The Cub Scout motto that he'd lived with forever, since he was a kid.

"On your marks!" the starter yelled.

At last, this was it. Harry's chance to win a gold medal in an important world-class meet.

"Get set." Harry knelt with one knee on the track. His foot on the starting block. Tense. Waiting. He pulled in a breath …

"Go!" He pushed off with all his strength. Exploding out of the blocks.

Eyes on the finish line. Legs like pistons. Feet hammering the track.

But smooth. Smooth. Keep the arms smooth, elbows tucked in. Relaxed. Waste no energy. All the power to the legs.

Go. Go. Go. Eyes on the finish line.

There it was.

His chest hit the tape.

But right beside him was Robinson. And just behind him, Edwin Roberts.

Almost before it started, but after an eternity had passed, the race was over. The crowd erupted into cheers and yells.

But who had won?

Harry jogged out, then stopped. Wiping sweat from his eyes on his shirt, he glanced back. Was it him? Or was it Robinson?

The officials consulted, shaking their heads.

Valerie left the stands and hurried to Harry's side, eyes questioning.

"I think I got it," he whispered to her. But he wasn't certain.

News photographers and reporters swarmed the field, spraying Harry and Robinson with questions.

"How do you feel?"

"Think you came first?"

Harry shook his head. He just didn't know for sure.

They'd have to wait for the official announcement up on the giant scoreboard after the officials had consulted the photos of the finish.

Harry stood with Valerie, out of the blazing direct sunlight in a bit of shade on the runway leading out of the stadium. Newsmen surrounded them. But they were silent now. Waiting.

After fifteen minutes of agonizing silence, the public address system sputtered.

Valerie grabbed Harry's arm …

But it was just the announcement for another race.

More minutes crawled by. Harry's mouth was dry. He asked for a drink. Would this be it? Had he finally won Gold? It was as if his whole lifetime was focused on this field, this one event, this very moment.

From the time he was a little kid Cub Scout and helping build up those dikes against the Red River flood, that night so many years ago in St. Boniface. The move to North Vancouver, his troubles growing up in an inhospitable community, the unfriendly schools. He thought about his paper route, where he got his time sprinting around his route to under an hour.

And his competitive running. The ecstasy of winning races, setting world records. The agony of the crushing defeats in the Rome Olympics in 1960 and the British Empire Games in Perth in 1962.

The crowd waited in hushed silence while the officials continued to examine the photographs of the finish and argue.

Finally, after forty-two minutes, the loudspeakers crackled.

"Thank you for your patience, ladies and gentlemen. The officials have studied the photos of the 100-yard dash, and they have concluded that the winner of the 100-yard dash with a time of 9.4 seconds is ..." the announcer paused "... Harry Jerome for Canada."

"Yes!" Harry exploded, fists punching the sky.

His sister hugged him and burst into tears. Canadian fans in the bleachers cheered and hugged each other.

At last! At last. Harry had won the gold medal in a major competition. After all these years, he could now hold his head high. Finally, he was a champion. Finally.

Robinson lowered his head in disappointment but quickly recovered. He strolled over to Harry and shook his hand. "Congrats, man. Congrats."

"Thanks, man. Thanks a lot." Harry couldn't contain his grin.

The truth was that Harry had waited not forty-two minutes, but his whole life of unimaginable struggle to step onto the podium and receive that gold medal.

He had been a world-class sprinter all his track life, and held world records for both the 100 yards and the 100 meters sprints that were to last for eight years.

But until that day, this Canadian railway porter's son had never before achieved the triumph and deep personal satisfaction that comes from the victory at a major international meet like the British Empire and Commonwealth Games.

It was the best 9.4 seconds of Harry's life.

AFTERWORD

That day was the apex of Harry Jerome's career as a world-class sprinter. Even though the following year, at the 1967 Pan American Games in Winnipeg, in the 100 meters on a wet track, he slipped into a puddle at the finish line and fell on his face, he still came in first. Another gold medal to add to his collection.

Then, the next year at the Olympics in Mexico, he ran the 100 meters but didn't place in the medals. At age 28, he announced his retirement. Quite old for a sprinter.

Harry then turned his energies to developing programs to encourage physical fitness in young people. By this time, he'd become accustomed to dealing with the media. He became an excellent spokesperson for the importance of physical education programs for all youths, especially for young people who might be underprivileged because of their race or economic background. He knew from personal experience that if you develop an interest in a sports program when you are young, chances are it will carry on as you grow up and you'll be a much healthier adult. He was convinced that it was sports and athletics that got him through a difficult time growing up.

In 1969, Harry was asked by Prime Minister Pierre Trudeau to work to establish fitness programs for youth and amateur sports across Canada. Then two years later, Harry worked to create the Premier's Sports Award Program in British Columbia. It was a physical education resource program designed to help teachers and community instructors teach children basic sports skills and encourage their participation.

In 1970, Harry had the honor of being invited to Ottawa by Governor General Roland Michener to become an Officer of the Order of Canada. This was "in recognition of his achievements in track and field events in Canada and abroad and for his services to fitness in Canada."

In 1971, he was inducted into Canada's Sports Hall of Fame.

Also that year, he was declared to be the "B.C. athlete of the Century, 1871-1971."

Sadly, on November 28, 1982, at the young age of 42, Harry Jerome died suddenly of what is thought to have been a brain aneurism.

But the fame of his life lives on. The Harry Jerome Community Recreation Centre, not far from the site of Harry's high school in North Vancouver, bears his name. As does the Harry Jerome Sports Centre in North Burnaby. The Harry Jerome International Track Classic is held annually, in honor of the man whose talent and tenacity on and off the track inspired generations of Canadians to "never give up" in their own struggles for excellence.

Every year in Toronto since 1983, the Canadian Black Business and Professionals Association holds a dinner, honoring prominent members of the Canadian Black community. That evening, scholarships are awarded to promising young athletes and students. In honor of this great athlete's memory, the evening is called the Harry Jerome Awards.

Harry was an outstanding athlete who challenged the racial discrimination of his times. His life serves as a role model for Canadian youth, inspiring them in the power of believing in yourself and your dreams. And in always doing your best.

If ever you happen to stroll through Vancouver's beautiful Stanley Park, you will find near Brockton Oval, where Harry spent so much of his teenage life training, a splendid nine-foot-tall bronze statue depicting a magnificent athlete in full flight, striving for that finish line, striving to win Gold.

That athlete is Harry Jerome. The kid who grew up in North Vancouver.

A kid who overcame tremendous hardships in his life to become the fastest man on earth.

ACKNOWLEDGEMENTS

I owe an enormous debt of gratitude to Valerie Jerome, Harry's sister, Paul Winn, Harry's lifelong friend, and John Minichiello, Harry's coach, for their generosity in answering my many questions about Harry's life and achievements and for sharing their stories.

I also consulted Fil Fraser's book about Harry, titled *Running Uphill*, published in 2006 by Dragon Hill Publishing Ltd., for details about Harry's many accomplishments and challenges.

Thanks to my editor, Peter Carver, for his eagle eyes and probing questions.

Also thanks to Access Copyright for their funding for this project.

As well, thank you to my writing pals, Linda Bailey and Beryl Young, who embarked on this writing journey with me and provided much encouragement along the way.

And last, many thanks to Brian and the rest of my family for their continuing inspiration and support for this writing project.

INTERVIEW WITH NORMA CHARLES

How did you gain access to the detailed information about Harry's youth?

I met with Valerie Jerome, Harry's sister, whom I've known for many years. She generously provided me with information about her brother and their family and the life they shared, from the time they lived in St. Boniface, then moved to North Vancouver, as well as the life in track that they both experienced. She said she was happy I was writing a book about her brother that would be shared with young people across Canada.

I also met with Paul Winn who was Harry's best friend from about the age of sixteen when Paul moved west to North Vancouver and met Harry in high school. They shared a keen interest in sports—in particular, track and field—and he became Harry's running mate over the years. John Minichiello, Harry's coach and friend, also generously shared information about Harry and told me what it was like to coach this gifted and determined athlete. As well as checking information on the Internet about Harry, I consulted the extensive archives about Harry and Valerie held in Simon Fraser University's special collections. Then, to fill in the gaps, I used information from Fil Fraser's excellent book, *Running Uphill, the Fast Short Life of Canadian Champion Harry Jerome* (Dragon Hill Publishing Ltd. 2006).

What were the challenges for you as a writer in telling a story that focuses on the life of a real historical figure?

There must always be challenges in balancing fact and fiction in creating a story based on someone's life. I wanted this book to be dramatic and interesting for a young reader, but I also wanted it to be factually accurate. But there were plenty of occasions while writing the book when I just didn't know exactly what the weather was on a given day, what the names of Harry's various friends were, what he was wearing, eating, reading, what he was thinking. So I had to draw upon my own experiences of growing up in a family around the same era, close to the same neighborhood.

There are many parallels between Harry's life and mine. My family lived in Fort Garry, another Winnipeg suburb, and we moved west to Maillardville, British Columbia, not far from

North Vancouver, around the same time that the Jerome family moved—also to avoid the annual flooding of the Red River. Years later, my husband was a sprinter at UBC who competed against Harry in track meets around Vancouver. We were great fans of Harry's career. And our four children, growing up in Vancouver, were all keen athletes and enjoyed track and field.

But in the end, this book is a work of fiction, even though it's based on the life of someone I have come to greatly admire.

It seems that the Jerome family suffered less racial discrimination in St. Boniface than in North Vancouver. Is that true, and what is the explanation for the difference?
Yes, you're right that it does seem so. I think at the time, St. Boniface was a much more cosmopolitan area with people who'd come there from all over the world. Residents of St. Boniface were not only French, but also Ukrainian and Polish, and included a sizeable population of African Canadian families who lived there because of the proximity of the train station where many worked as porters.

In the 1950s and 60s, North Vancouver was populated mainly by people from Britain. In fact, there is still an area called "British Properties" where, at that time, you could not buy a house unless you or your ancestors were from Britain. I must say that this is not so today. The resident population is now as diverse as any other region on the west coast.

At the time of Harry's serious injury in the Common-wealth Games in Australia, Canada did not yet have a government-supported Medicare. This means Dr. Gillespie was extremely generous for not charging for the complicated operation he carried out to repair Harry's damaged leg. Tell us about their subsequent friendship.

When John Minichiello told me about Dr. Hector Gillespie's not charging for the operation on Harry's leg, and the doctor saying that he felt it was a privilege to have worked on such an outstanding athlete, John was so moved that he had tears in his eyes. And this was fifty years later. I don't know the details of Harry and Dr. Gillespie's subsequent friendship. But I've read that they remained friends up to the time of Harry's death in 1982, and that Dr. Gillespie encouraged Harry to return to running after the cast on his leg was removed six months after the operation. Dr. Gillespie died on Nov. 19, 2000, aged 82.